P9-CQN-674

PROPHECIES & END-TIME SPECULATIONS

The Shape of Things to Come

RELIGION & MODERN CULTURE
Title List

Born-Again Believers: Evangelicals and Charismatics

Color, Culture, and Creed: How Ethnic Background Influences Belief

The Controversial World of Biblical Archaeology:
Tomb Raiders, Fakes, and Scholars

The Grail, the Shroud, and Other Religious Relics:
Secrets and Ancient Mysteries

The Growth of North American Religious Beliefs: Spiritual Diversity

Issues of Church, State, and Religious Liberties:
Whose Freedom, Whose Faith?

Jesus, Fads, and the Media: The Passion and Popular Culture

Lost Gospels and Hidden Codes: New Concepts of Scripture

The Popularity of Meditation and Spiritual Practices:
Seeking Inner Peace

Prophecies and End-Time Speculations: The Shape of Things to Come

Touching the Supernatural World: Angels, Miracles, and Demons

When Religion and Politics Mix:
How Matters of Faith Influence Political Policies

Women and Religion: Reinterpreting Scriptures
to Find the Sacred Feminine

PROPHECIES & END-TIME SPECULATIONS
The Shape of Things to Come

by Kenneth McIntosh, M.Div.

Mason Crest Publishers
Philadelphia

Mason Crest Publishers Inc.
370 Reed Road
Broomall, Pennsylvania 19008
(866) MCP-BOOK (toll free)

First printing
1 2 3 4 5 6 7 8 9 10

Library of Congress Cataloging-in-Publication Data

McIntosh, Kenneth, 1959–
Prophecies & end-time speculations : the shape of things to come / by Kenneth R. McIntosh.
p. cm. — (Religion and modern culture)
Includes bibliographical references and index.
ISBN 1-59084-979-5 (alk. paper) ISBN 1-59084-970-1 (series)
1. End of the world—Juvenile literature. 2. Prophecies—Juvenile literature. I. Title: Prophecies and end-time speculations. II. Title. III. Series.
BT877.M35 2005
202'.3—dc22

2005012951

Produced by Harding House Publishing Service, Inc.
www.hardinghousepages.com
Interior design by Dianne Hodack.
Cover design by MK Bassett-Harvey.
Printed in India.

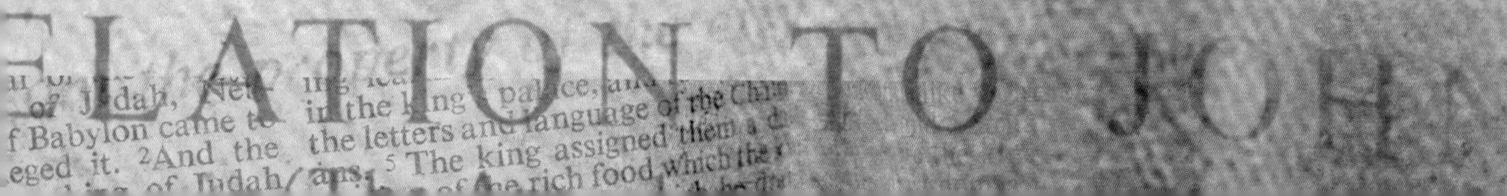

CONTENTS

Introduction 6

1. The End Is All Over 8

2. Ancient Prophecies 18

3. A History of the End 30

4. Doomsday Cults 44

5. Native Visions & the New Age 62

6. Pop Culture Apocalypse 72

7. Revelation Revisited 94

Further Reading 108

For More Information 109

Index 110

Picture Credits 111

Biographies 112

INTRODUCTION

by Dr. Marcus J. Borg

You are about to begin an important and exciting experience: the study of modern religion. Knowing about religion—and religions—is vital for understanding our neighbors, whether they live down the street or across the globe.

Despite the modern trend toward religious doubt, most of the world's population continues to be religious. Of the approximately six billion people alive today, around two billion are Christians, one billion are Muslims, 800 million are Hindus, and 400 million are Buddhists. Smaller numbers are Sikhs, Shinto, Confucian, Taoist, Jewish, and indigenous religions.

Religion plays an especially important role in North America. The United States is the most religious country in the Western world: about 80 percent of Americans say that religion is "important" or "very important" to them. Around 95 percent say they believe in God. These figures are very different in Europe, where the percentages are much smaller. Canada is "in between": the figures are lower than for the United States, but significantly higher than in Europe. In Canada, 68 percent of citizens say religion is of "high importance," and 81 percent believe in God or a higher being.

The United States is largely Christian. Around 80 percent describe themselves as Christian. In Canada, professing Christians are 77 percent of the population. But religious diversity is growing. According to Harvard scholar Diana Eck's recent book *A New Religious America*, the United States has recently become the most religiously diverse country in the world. Canada is also a country of great religious variety.

Fifty years ago, religious diversity in the United States meant Protestants, Catholics, and Jews, but since the 1960s, immigration from Asia, the Middle East, and Africa has dramatically increased the number of people practicing other religions. There are now about six million Muslims, four million Buddhists, and a million Hindus in the United States. To compare these figures to two historically important Protestant denominations in the United States, about 3.5 million are Presbyterians and 2.5 million are Episcopalians. There are more Buddhists in the United States than either of these denominations, and as many Muslims as the two denominations combined. This means that knowing about other religions is not just knowing about people in other parts of the world—but about knowing people in our schools, workplaces, and neighborhoods.

Moreover, religious diversity does not simply exist between religions. It is found within Christianity itself:

- There are many different forms of Christian worship. They range from Quaker silence to contemporary worship with rock music to traditional liturgical worship among Catholics and Episcopalians to Pentecostal enthusiasm and speaking in tongues.

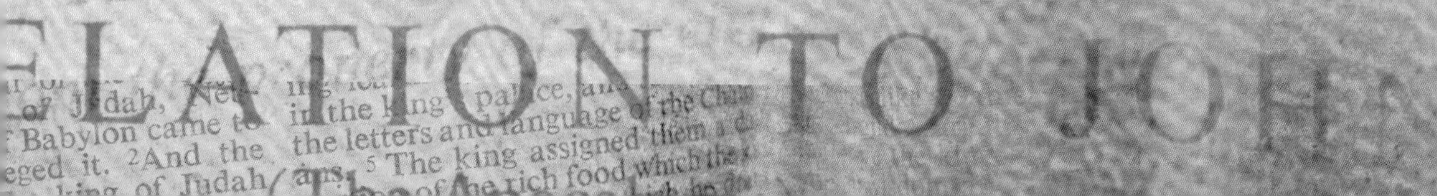

- Christians are divided about the importance of an afterlife. For some, the next life—a paradise beyond death—is their primary motive for being Christian. For other Christians, the afterlife does not matter nearly as much. Instead, a relationship with God that transforms our lives this side of death is the primary motive.
- Christians are divided about the Bible. Some are biblical literalists who believe that the Bible is to be interpreted literally and factually as the inerrant revelation of God, true in every respect and true for all time. Other Christians understand the Bible more symbolically as the witness of two ancient communities—biblical Israel and early Christianity—to their life with God.

Christians are also divided about the role of religion in public life. Some understand "separation of church and state" to mean "separation of religion and politics." Other Christians seek to bring Christian values into public life. Some (commonly called "the Christian Right") are concerned with public policy issues such as abortion, prayer in schools, marriage as only heterosexual, and pornography. Still other Christians name the central public policy issues as American imperialism, war, economic injustice, racism, health care, and so forth. For the first group, values are primarily concerned with individual behavior. For the second group, values are also concerned with group behavior and social systems. The study of religion in North America involves not only becoming aware of other religions but also becoming aware of differences within Christianity itself. Such study can help us to understand people with different convictions and practices.

And there is one more reason why such study is important and exciting: religions deal with the largest questions of life. These questions are intellectual, moral, and personal. Most centrally, they are:

- What is real? The religions of the world agree that "the real" is more than the space-time world of matter and energy.
- How then shall we live?
- How can we be "in touch" with "the real"? How can we connect with it and become more deeply centered in it?

This series will put you in touch with other ways of seeing reality and how to live.

Chapter 1

THE END IS ALL OVER

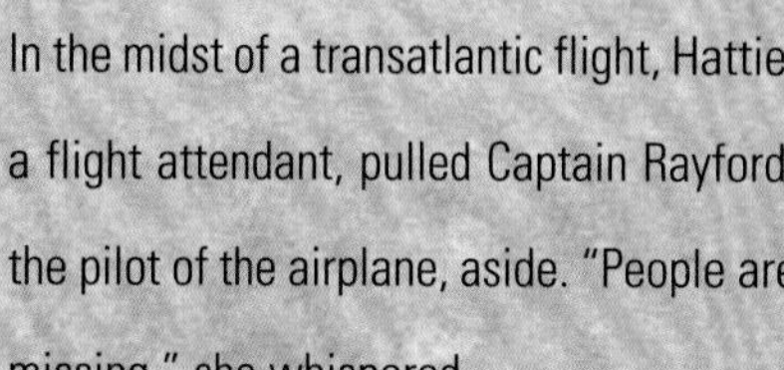

In the midst of a transatlantic flight, Hattie, a flight attendant, pulled Captain Rayford, the pilot of the airplane, aside. "People are missing," she whispered.

"What do you mean?"

"A whole bunch of people, just gone!"

Indeed, a great number of people had vanished into thin air. Not only on this 747 flying over the Atlantic Ocean, but throughout the entire world millions of people vanished. All infants and children had suddenly and mysteriously disappeared. Some adults were missing—but others were not. What had happened?

Days later, Captain Rayford found a videotape message explaining the mysterious phenomenon: "Every person who believed in . . . Jesus Christ . . . all such people were literally taken from the earth, leaving everything material behind." This event, in which believers are taken from the earth, is called the Rapture from the Greek word meaning "caught up." The tape explains that little children in their innocence, along with adult believers, have disappeared in the Rapture.

THE "LEFT BEHIND" PHENOMENA

These events take place in one of the best-selling novels of all time, *Left Behind.* The series of books by that title, written by authors Tim LaHaye and Jerry B. Jenkins, have sold over sixty-two million copies and inspired a movie and television series. According to an article in *Newsweek*, one out of eight Americans has read a book in the *Left Behind* series. Critics do not regard their novels as great literature, but Tim LaHaye and Jerry Jenkins are America's best-selling authors. They are evangelical Christians: people who say they have a personal relationship with Christ and who regard the Bible as an authority for life.

The *Left Behind* books are based on apocalyptic portions of the Bible. The word *apocalypse* is Greek for "revelation." Apocalyptic books—such as the book of Revelation in the Christian New Testament—claim to reveal God's plans for the future.

END-TIME FASCINATION

The *Left Behind* books aren't the only example of America's fascination with the end of time. You do not have to be a Christian—or even religious—to be fascinated with doomsday scenarios or promises of the world's imminent end. In fact, the end times are all over—they are all over the place.

GLOSSARY

Holy Grail: According to legend, the cup said to have been used by Jesus at the Last Supper, and by Joseph of Arimathea to collect Jesus's blood and sweat at the crucifixion.

Maya calendar: A complex calendar created by the ancient Maya based on astrology and mathematics.

Nostradamus: A widely read prophet of the sixteenth century.

For instance, as you surf the World Wide Web, a pop-up advertisement may appear on your screen showing an animated picture of tidal waves sweeping across a major city in the United States. The ad is promoting *The Day After Tomorrow,* a movie released on DVD in 2005. The film presents a nonreligious view of the end of history, a time when global warming caused by pollution will bring life as we know it to a crashing finale.

Or maybe you're hanging out at a local coffee shop where a Native American band is playing. In the middle of one song, the singer talks about things that are happening today. He believes Native people of his age are the promised Seventh Generation—the generation prophesied by American Indian spiritual leaders more than a century ago. The Seventh Generation signals the end of time when Native people will lead in healing the Earth and restoring a sense of balance to society.

It's the end of the world as we know it.
It's the end of the world as we know it.
It's the end of the world as we know it. . . .
And I feel fine!

—*"It's the End of the World as We Know It (And I Feel Fine)" by R.E.M.*

Browsing the shelves at your local bookstore, you'll find all manner of books about end-time predictions: a series of books for teens based on the *Left Behind* novels, numerous nonfiction books claiming to detail prophetic predictions based on the Bible, and books from other spiritual perspectives predicting what lies ahead. ***Nostradamus***'s prophecies continue to fascinate readers, along with the predictions made by the psychic Edgar Cayce. The *Celestine Prophecy* is a best-selling novel that expresses the beliefs of a new emerging spirituality. Writers see the ***Holy Grail***, the pyramids of Egypt, and even the ancient ***Maya calendar*** as prophetic clues revealing end-time events.

WHY ARE WE OBSESSED WITH THE END?

Why are so many people fascinated by end-time prophecies? Richard Abanes, a noted expert on cults and religious beliefs, writes in his book *End-Time Visions*:

> The truth is that most people want to see into the future. There is nothing as disconcerting as facing the unknown. . . . For some people, confronting an unending series of tomorrows filled with uncertainty is unendurable. Hence, they invent a future scenario that is full of set expectations . . . with this mindset; they know exactly what is coming.

HOW MANY END-TIME BELIEVERS?

In May 2004, a *Newsweek* survey reported the following results:

- 36 percent of Americans believe the book of Revelation contains "true prophecy." A larger group, 47 percent, say the book is "metaphorical" in nature.
- 55 percent of Americans believe "the faithful will be taken up to heaven in the Rapture."
- 17 percent of Americans say the world will end in their lifetime.

Of course, most people would not say they "invent" their beliefs regarding the end times. They believe they receive their beliefs from scriptures or traditions.

DATE SETTING—A SAD EXAMPLE

In the Bible, Jesus says, "About that day and hour no one knows, neither the angels of heaven, nor the Son, but only the Father" (Matthew 24:36). Despite this clear statement regarding the unknowable date, some people have set dates for Christ's return. The results can be unfortunate.

S. petrus
maria virgine
thomas
S. matheus
Credo in spiritum
sanctum
Sanctam ecclesiam catholicam
peccatorum
S. Judas
S. mathias
S. Simon

"I delight greatly in the New Jerusalem, not because it has a street of pure gold . . . but because there will be the presence of the Lord and the absence of any more tears. The New Jerusalem is coming soon and this world will pass instantly away. . . . Thank God for the prospect of no more tears forever."

—Watchman Nee, a Chinese Christian who lived through government persecution

For example, in 1992, a young man was very excited about the coming Rapture. He wore a bright shirt that said in big letters, "Jesus Is Coming, October 28, 1992!" The boy and his family were part of Los Angeles Maranatha Mission Church, and his folks drove around in a station wagon with a huge bright banner proclaiming the same message. They followed the teachings of "prophet" Lee Jang Rim, a Korean minister who had announced this date to his followers.

In mid-October, the boy grew more and more excited. His family had sold their business and emptied their bank accounts so they could spend the money telling people to be ready. After all, they would have no need for money in a few weeks, and they wanted everyone to be ready when the Rapture came.

There was incredible disappointment at the Maranatha Mission Church building in Los Angeles when midnight of October 28 came and went. Some members of the Mission Church wept hysterically. Others sat stonelike, in shock. The young man and his family had a rough time starting life again with their business and savings gone.

Life didn't turn out so well for the "prophet," Lee Jang Rim, either. Korean police arrested him for defrauding his followers out of 4.4 million dollars. He had invested a large part of the money in bonds that would pay off in May of 1993—six months *after* his predicted Rapture would come. It seems this self-proclaimed prophet was mostly concerned with profit.

This book contains accounts of date-setters, frauds, and—worst of all—doomsday prophets who lead their followers to tragic deaths. These people are the "dark side" of belief in end-time prophecy. Such people, however, are only a fraction of prophecy believers. The great majority of religious people hold balanced and healthy beliefs regarding the end times. For millions, the promise of a coming future Kingdom provides hope and guidance for life today.

CANADIAN APOCALYPSE—NOT SO SURE

Religion has less influence on Canadian culture than on that of the United States. Sixty-eight percent of U.S. citizens say religion is "very important" in their life, compared with 41 percent of their neighbors to the north. In the United States, the largest Protestant group is the conservative Southern Baptist Church, whereas the dominant Protestant denominations in Canada are the more liberal United Churches of Canada and the Anglican Church of Canada. It is not surprising, therefore, that Canadians are less expectant regarding Bible prophecy. The Taylor Nelson Sofres Intersearch (TNS) Millennium Study surveyed a thousand Canadians and a thousand citizens of the United States. The study found that 42 percent of U.S. residents agreed with the statement, "Revelation events will occur." By contrast, only 17 percent of Canadians agreed with the statement.

Chapter 2

ANCIENT PROPHECIES

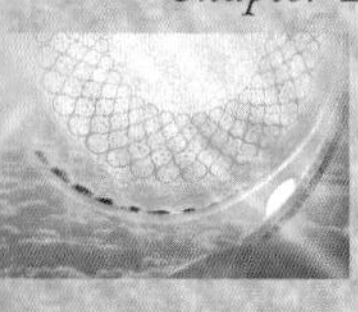

Stepping into the Dome of the Rock is an unforgettable experience. Because it is a sacred shrine, visitors must leave their shoes outside the door. The floor is covered with thick Persian carpets that muffle sounds beneath the vast dome. A million tiny pieces of precious metals, wood, and ivory combine to create vast and dazzling patterns on the walls. Muslims call this place the *Haram el-Sharif*, "the Noble Sanctuary." For Jews, it is the Temple Mount where God promised his presence would abide forever. For Christians, it is a place closely associated with the return of Jesus Christ.

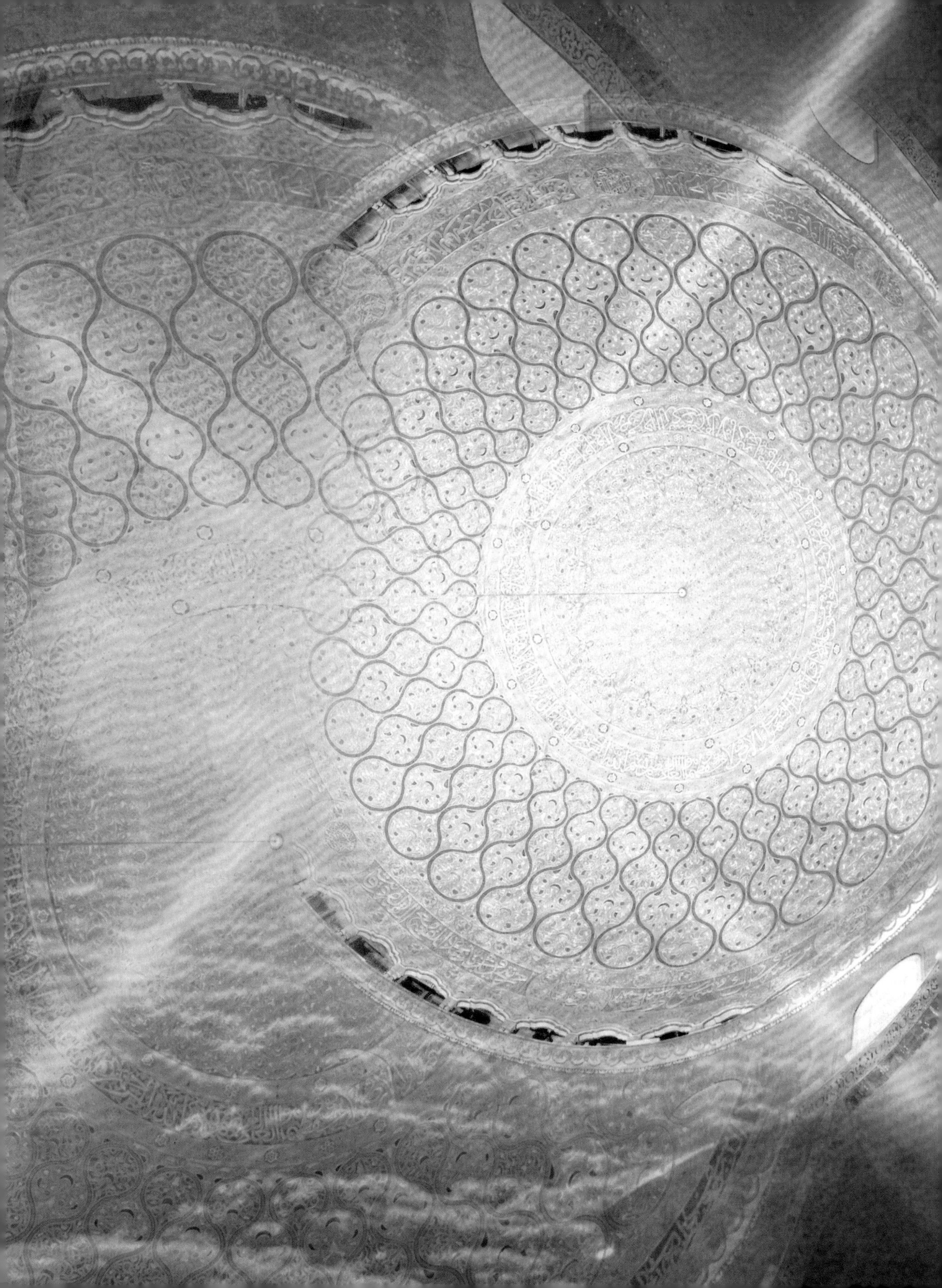

The center of this stunning, ornate shrine is a large rock surface, perhaps forty feet (12 meters) across. According to Jews, Christians, and Muslims, this bare, rugged stone is one of the holiest places on earth: the top of Mount Moriah, where God asked Abraham to sacrifice his beloved son. All three faiths agree on this point.

According to Judaism, the rock is also the exact location of the Holy of Holies, which was a part of Solomon's temple. This is where the ***Ark of the Covenant*** sat. The Holy of Holies was so sacred that ordinary mortals dared not enter it for fear of their lives. Readers may recall the end of the movie *Raiders of the Lost Ark*, in which the Nazis learned not to mess with that ark.

Islam also holds sacred traditions about this place. Muslims believe Mohammed ascended to heaven from this rock. The Noble Sanctuary is regarded as the center of the world in Muslim geography.

The Dome of the Rock is overwhelming, sacred, and holy. It may also be the most bitterly contested site on the planet. ***Hassidic*** Jews believe the temple of God must be rebuilt on its former location before the Jewish people can achieve their destiny. Some Christians believe the temple must be rebuilt before Jesus can return. Muslims are, of course, unwilling to simply give their holy site to Christians and Jews.

So three great faiths contend bitterly for one small plot of land in the midst of the Holy Land. Security there is tight, because fanatical groups might attempt to blow up the dome. Believers in three differing traditions each have plans for the same holy site—and each is unwilling to yield. The dispute is so bitter that it has caused bloodshed. Disagreement over who will control the site has caused peace talks between Israel and Palestine to break down.

These ongoing conflicts over the Dome of the Rock demonstrate the continuing influence of ancient scriptures. Even in a world with superfast computers and high-tech gadgets, age-old prophetic words control the hearts of millions of people.

GLOSSARY

Ark of the Covenant: The chest in which, according to biblical accounts, Moses placed the Ten Commandments.

Hassidic: Having the characteristics of a member of a Jewish mystical sect founded in Poland around 1750.

transliterated: Represented a letter or word written in one alphabet using the corresponding letter of another alphabet so that the sound of the letter or word remained the same.

Tribulation: Seven years of great difficulty, affliction, and distress predicted in the book of Revelation.

APOCALYPTIC BOOKS

The Bible is actually a collection of short books written over many centuries. Hebrew writers produced the Old Testament, which comprises much of the Torah, the Jewish scripture. Christians wrote the New Testament in Greek. Due to a disagreement between Christians about what should be included in the Bible, Catholic Bibles have seventy-three books and Protestant Bibles sixty-six.

"Arguments about Scripture achieve nothing but a stomach-ache and a headache."

—Tertullian, the great African theologian who lived 160–220 CE

A few of the books in the Bible are apocalyptic, including Isaiah, Daniel, and Revelation. These apocalyptic books describe the future in symbolic language. The book of Revelation is perhaps the most fascinating yet confusing book of the Bible.

THE BOOK OF REVELATION

The author of this book calls himself "John." He is generally thought to be the Apostle John, one of Jesus's twelve disciples (although not all Bible scholars agree on this). John says he received a series of visions when he was "on the island of Patmos for the Word of God." (Patmos was a small island in the Aegean Sea used as a prison colony by Rome.) Whoever John was, he wrote at a time when Romans were torturing and killing Christians.

Some scholars believe the book of Revelation was written in coded language to protect those who delivered it. If authorities found a Christian carrying a book that in plain language urged resistance to the emperor, they would probably kill the Christian. Using expressions like "Babylon" to represent Rome and "the Beast" to represent the Roman emperor, the book of Revelation may have served as a coded message of resistance.

According to the book, Jesus appeared to John in a vision and instructed John to record a series of visions. First, Christ gives letters for seven churches in Asia. John is then allowed a peek into heaven where a vast multiracial crowd worships Jesus. Willing to die for Christ, these people now live with him.

ANCIENT PROPHECIES

The Old Testament

LETTERS TO NUMBERS

The Old Testament was written in Hebrew and the New Testament in Greek. Both of these languages are "dual character systems," meaning that each letter stands for both a sound and a number. Gematria is the calculation of the numerical equivalence of letters, words, or phrases to gain an insight into the relationships between words and ideas. Two words with the same numerical value are considered equal.

The first ten letters of the Greek and Hebrew alphabets are numbered 1, 2, 3, and so on. From ten through eighty in the Greek alphabet, and through ninety in the Hebrew, the numerical equivalents go by tens: 20, 30, 40, to 100. The remainder of the alphabets progress by hundreds, 800 in the Greek alphabet and 400 in Hebrew.

The Hebrew word *chai* means life; in Hebrew it is spelled with only two letters, *chet* and *yod*. Chet has a numerical value of eight, and the yod's numerical value is ten, for a total word value of eighteen. Monetary gifts for special occasions are often given in amounts equal to chai: $18, $36, $180.

"Behold, I am coming soon, bringing my reward, to repay everyone for what he has done. I am the Alpha and the Omega, the first and the last, the beginning and the end."

—Jesus, from the last chapter of Revelation

Chapter 13 of Revelation introduces the horrifying villain known as "the Beast" or "the Antichrist." Many Bible scholars believe this is the Emperor Nero. The beast has a famous number—666, although some ancient copies of Revelation read 616 rather than 666. "Caesar Nero," ***transliterated*** into Hebrew, has the numeric value of 666, and in Latin letters the value of 616. Therefore, Nero fits both versions. Nero was the first emperor to torture and kill Christians. He ordered people to kill his mother and to cut off the head of his first wife. He kicked his second wife to death while she was pregnant. He lit Christians on fire for a spectacle. "Beast" would be an appropriate description of his character.

Chapter 17 introduces another evil character, "the great city Babylon," portrayed as a drunken woman riding on a seven-headed dragon. The woman sits upon "seven mountains," and she is "the great city which has dominion over the kings of the earth." Many Bible scholars believe "Babylon" is a code name for Imperial Rome, a city famous for its seven hills; Rome certainly did rule over the earth in John's time.

The final chapters of Revelation present a series of bright and beautiful visions, like fireworks going off at the end of a game. Choirs in heaven shout "Hallelujah!" Christ rides in glory as the King of Kings on a great white horse. He casts Satan into a lake of fire and judges the dead. The New Jerusalem descends from heaven, with God in the midst of the heavenly city, living alongside human beings. "And night shall be no more; they need no light of lamp or sun, for the Lord God shall be their light, and they shall reign forever and ever" (Revelation 21:5, NRSV).

REVELATION

REJECTED REVELATIONS

In addition to the apocalyptic books in the Bible today, a number of prophetic books in the ancient world were not included in scripture. Jewish and Christian leaders in ancient times rejected these because they did not believe God genuinely inspired them. Some of these rejected books bore false authors—writers who claimed to be the Old Testament Enoch or the Apostle Peter. The rejected apocalyptic books also showed a morbid preoccupation with hell and judgment.

Throughout the centuries, Bible readers have taken various approaches to understanding Revelation. The description on page 26 focuses on the historical setting in which the book was written—but many readers have interpreted Revelation as an outline of events that will take place in the future. They understand the ***Tribulation,*** Antichrist, and so on as unfulfilled end-time events. Yet others have understood Revelation as a description of events unfolding through the long course of human history. Finally, there are those who understand the book as a symbolic statement applicable to life at every stage of human history.

Since Revelation contains such highly symbolic language, it has fueled endless speculation. In every age, people have "read into" the book the events of their time, along with their fears and prejudices. It has been a source of great comfort—and great fear.

Chapter 3

A HISTORY OF THE END

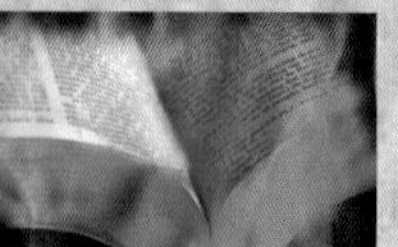

"Repent! Repent! The Day of Judgment is nigh. Only the righteous will inherit the earth. We alone shall survive the fiery judgment that is about to sweep over the world. Yet we must be pure! Only the pure shall stand before God. Do you have wealth? Give it away, now—free yourself from the sins of greed. Have you been reading worldly amusements? Bring your impure books to the fire and burn them. Prepare! Be ready for the day of the Lord."

It was the year 1535, and the self-proclaimed prophet, Jan van Leyden, had taken control of the German city of Münster. Followers of Leyden and another preacher, Jan Matthys, were known as ***millennialists***.

Revelation chapter 20 describes a thousand-year time when Christ will reign on earth. For centuries, preachers had taught these verses as symbolic. The two Jans, however, preached a literal kingdom with Christ physically ruling as king. They said the millennium was about to begin. Jan Matthys said he was the prophet Enoch, returned to bring the Kingdom.

Followers of Jan van Leyden and Jan Matthys took over the city of Münster. They forced citizens to "purify" themselves in anticipation of the second coming. They seized the wealth of the rich and burned all books except the Bible. When a blacksmith was openly skeptical of Matthys' preaching, the "prophet" announced the devil had possessed this blacksmith. A crowd tied up the unfortunate skeptic and stood him against a wall. Jan Matthys himself shot and killed the man.

Eventually, a Catholic army led by a bishop surrounded the city and demanded that the end-time fanatics surrender. They didn't; instead, their behavior became even more bizarre. Jan van Leyden ran naked across the city as a "prophetic sign." He also took a number of women as wives.

On May 25, 1535, the army attacked and quickly took control of Münster. The millennialist leaders were tortured to death with red-hot irons. The army hung their bodies in cages from the Münster church tower, where the iron cages still hang today.

The tragedy of Jan van Leyden, Jan Matthys, and Münster reminded Europeans that Bible prophecy could be dangerously misused. Yet it was not the first or last time prophecy madness would take place.

END-TIME EVENTS OF THE MIDDLE AGES

In the year 386, a brilliant African philosopher converted to Christianity. After years of playboy living, Augustine of Hippo found freedom from lust in the Christian faith. He then devoted himself to explaining Christian beliefs.

GLOSSARY

astrology: The study of the positions of the moon, sun, and planets in the belief that their motions affect human beings.

barbarians: People whose culture and behavior are considered uncivilized.

millennialists: People who believe in a thousand-year span of holiness spoken in Christian prophecy.

revivals: Meetings of evangelical Christians intended to awaken religious fervor in those who attend.

At the time when Augustine was writing, ***barbarians*** overran the city of Rome. A century before, Rome had officially adopted Christian beliefs. Now Christians asked, "What is going on? Is God still in charge of history?"

Augustine sought an answer from the book of Revelation. Revelation 20 spoke of Christ ruling on earth for a thousand years. Augustine said, "Christ is already ruling—within the hearts of believers." Even if barbarians conquered the Roman Empire, they could not conquer the rule of Christ within the church. Augustine said Christians should not confuse the Kingdom of God with earthly political power. For the next seven hundred years, most Christians supported Augustine's belief.

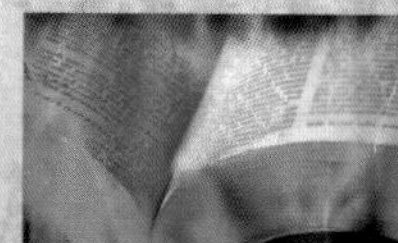

The Middle Ages, however, had their share of end-time mania. Historian Barbara Tuchman says the Black Death, which lasted from

"False prophets will appear."

—words of Jesus, in Matthew's Gospel

1347 to 1350, was "the most lethal disaster in recorded history." A third of Europe died. Societies broke down. Armed groups of robber-knights terrorized innocent citizens. It truly seemed like the time of plagues and horrors described in the book of Revelation.

In 1517, a young German monk named Martin Luther changed the shape of history by protesting policies of the Catholic Church. He began what historians call the Reformation. The Christian church split into Protestant and Catholic branches. Both Luther and the pope considered each other to be the Antichrist, and Europe was plunged into decades of religious wars. (It was during this time that the tragedy of Münster occurred.)

During the sixteenth century, a French astrologer named Nostradamus published a book titled *The Centuries.* It has generated interest—and controversy—ever since. As a young man, Nostradamus studied medicine in college; at that time, schools taught ***astrology*** as part of the medical science curriculum. Nostradamus began to work as a doctor, but he was traumatized by the death of his wife and children from the plague. After their death, he turned to astrology. At that time, there were some 30,000 fortune-tellers of various sorts in Paris. Despite plenty of competition, Nostradamus became the favorite astrologer of the queen of France.

Nostradamus wrote hundreds of vague poetic "prophecies" that have been interpreted as predictions of everything from the rise of Napoleon and Hitler to atomic war. One reason for his fame is his vagueness. Nostradamus's rhymes are so unclear, and there are so many, that one can read just about anything into them—after the fact. However, fans of Nostradamus have had extraordinarily poor luck actually predicting any events from his prophecies.

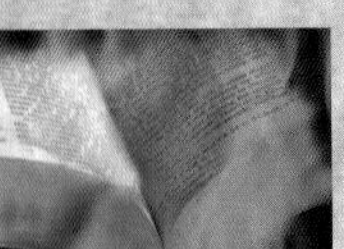

American history has also seen its share of prophetic speculations. In the 1700s and 1800s, a number of religious revivals took place on the American frontier. Huge crowds met to hear popular preachers. Thousands were converted, and significant moral and social reforms took place.

People called New York State in the early 1800s the "burned over district" because so many religious ***revivals*** took place there. In 1838, New York resident William Miller went public with his Bible prophecy ministry. He published a best-selling book titled *Evidence from Scripture and History of the Second Coming of Christ About the year 1843.* Miller was a skillful preacher, and he spoke to huge crowds throughout New England. Miller became even more popular in the predicted year of 1843. A spectacular comet, so bright people could see it in the daytime, added excitement to his movement. Then he predicted an exact date: Jesus would come on March 21, 1844.

America grew more and more excited as the day approached. Several wealthy businessmen sold their businesses and donated funds to Miller's preaching ministry. Farmers decided not to gather their harvest of corn and potatoes because "It was tempting [God] to store up grain for a season that would never arrive."

Historians refer to March 21, 1844, as "The Great Disappointment." One of Miller's followers, Hiram Edson, described the shock of that day's passing: "Our fondest hopes and expectations were blasted, and such a spirit of weeping came over us as I have never experienced before. We wept, and wept until the [next] day dawn." Miller retired from preaching and died in obscurity five years later.

The Great Disappointment was far from the last disappointment for millennial date setters. *The Watchtower Bible and Tract Society*, better known as the Jehovah's Witnesses, has a record of date setting. Their

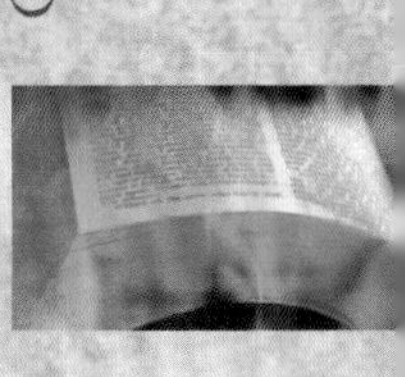

THE NOT-SO-AMAZING PROPHET NOSTRADAMUS

Publishers have greatly enhanced Nostradamus's fame by rewriting his prophecies after events occur. For example, a famous prophecy of Nostradamus says, "Beasts wild with hunger will cross the rivers, the greatest part of the battlefield will be against Hitler . . . when the Child of Germany observes no law." That sounds like an amazing prediction of Hitler and World War II. However, antique French copies of Nostradamus's book read very differently from today's popular English editions. In the original book, the name is "Ister" not Hitler. Furthermore, "Ister" is the "the child of Germaine" (a French name) rather than Germany. These changes are typical of the ways Nostradamus has been edited to bolster claims of amazing prophetic prediction. You can read more about this in Richard Abanes's book *End-Time Visions: The Doomsday Obsession.*

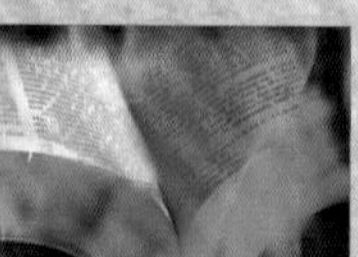

founder, Charles Taze Russell, was a popular prophecy teacher similar to William Miller. Russell first proclaimed 1873 for Christ's return. After the year came and went, he explained that Christ had in fact returned on the promised date—only he had done so invisibly. Russell then revised the date for a visible return to 1914. He based this date on measurements of the Great Pyramid in Egypt, which he called "God's Stone Witness." When 1914 came and went, Russell explained he had been short on his measurements—the end would come in 1915. After Russell died in 1917 (without Christ's return), Joseph Franklin Rutherford became president of the Jehovah's Witnesses; he predicted a 1925 date. The next prediction by the Jehovah's Witnesses suggested that in 1940, "Armageddon is very near." On September 15, 1941, the *Watchtower* referred to "remaining months before Armageddon." The *Watchtower* also suggested members should forsake marriage and avoid starting families in light of the soon-coming end. After World War II ended, the *Watchtower* predicted the second coming in 1975. Since missing that one, the Jehovah's Witnesses have refrained from setting dates.

RECENT PREDICTIONS

In the late twentieth century, Bible prophecy speculation increased even more. From the 1960s to 2000, predictions of the second coming have been made every few years. In the 1970s, evangelical Christian Hal Lindsey achieved remarkable sales success with a book titled *The Late Great Planet Earth.* According to Lindsay, Jesus promised to return within a generation of the reestablishment of Israel; Israel was established in 1948. A "generation" in the Bible is forty years. Readers can do the math.

The 1990s saw unprecedented interest in apocalyptic prophecy. The approach of the year 2000, coupled with the Bible's reference to "the

A HISTORY OF THE END

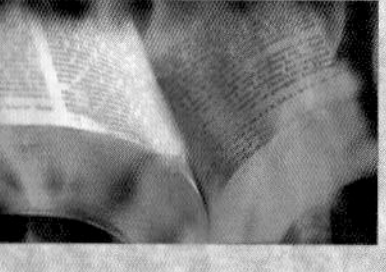

Y2K

"Blasted be the bones of those who calculate the end, for when the calculated time comes and Messiah does not appear, people despair of his ever coming."

—*Rabbi Jonathan*

millennium" in Revelation 20, fueled speculation. There was widespread fear over the alleged "Y2K bug," which would cause computer systems worldwide to crash. Some families stored up food supplies, electric generators, and even weapons to prepare for the predicted shutdown. Bible prophecy teachers hinted this could be the "Great Tribulation" accompanied by Jesus's rapture of his church. At midnight of 2000, people waited with baited breath. Other than a few practical jokes, nothing much happened. Computers still functioned, and Jesus still delayed his return.

At the beginning of the twenty-first century, as terrorism and wars increase worldwide fears, we are likely to hear yet more predictions of the world's end. We would do well to keep in mind the track record of previous predictions.

Chapter 4

DOOMSDAY CULTS

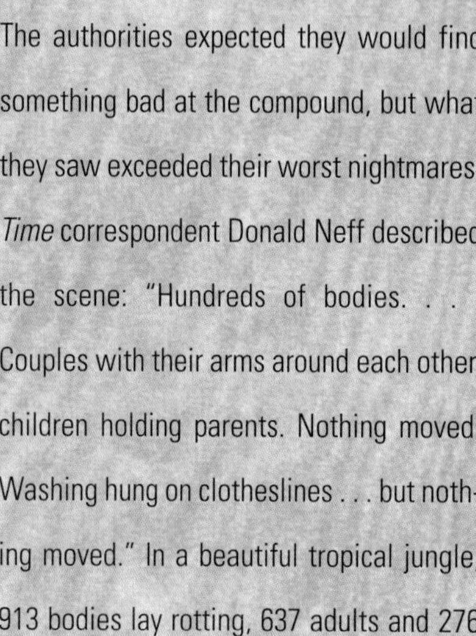

The authorities expected they would find something bad at the compound, but what they saw exceeded their worst nightmares. *Time* correspondent Donald Neff described the scene: "Hundreds of bodies. . . . Couples with their arms around each other, children holding parents. Nothing moved. Washing hung on clotheslines . . . but nothing moved." In a beautiful tropical jungle, 913 bodies lay rotting, 637 adults and 276 children. The People's Temple had come to an unbelievable, tragic end.

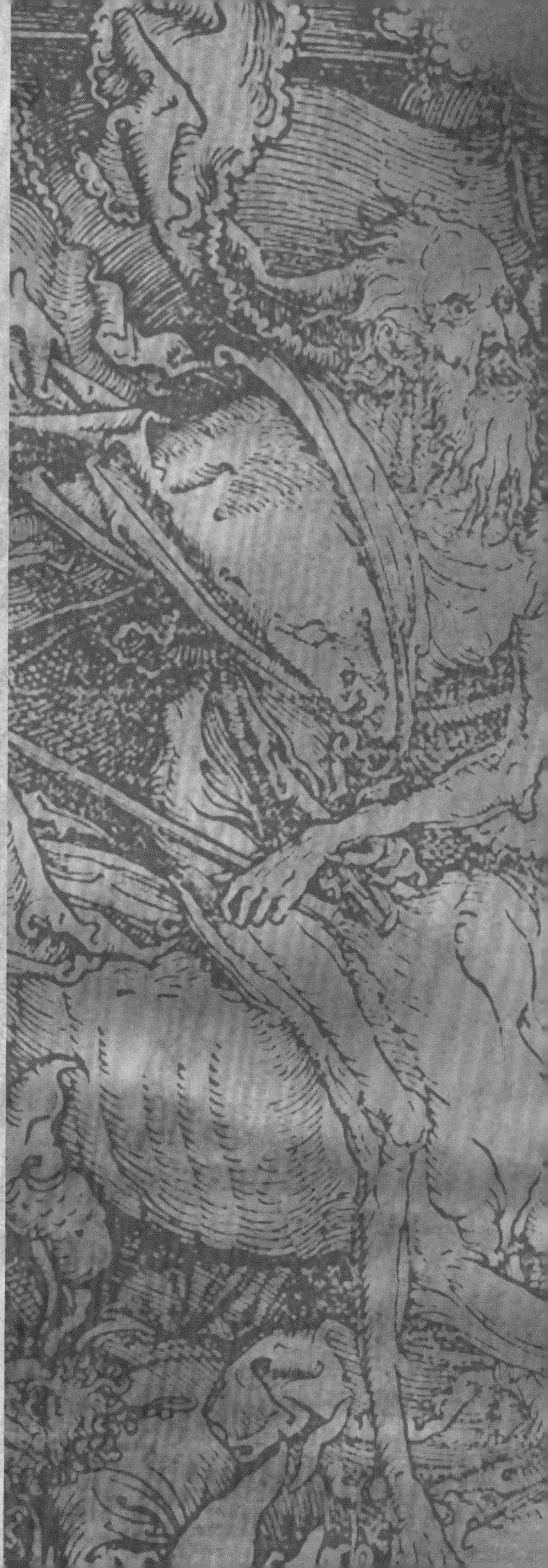

The story began twenty-two years earlier. James Warren Jones, better known as Jim Jones, held degrees from Indiana University and Butler University. He was an ordained pastor, who began his preaching career in a Methodist church. He soon left that church because blacks were not welcome there. In 1956, he began the Peoples Temple in his home state of Indiana. Nine years later, he moved the group to Redwood City, California.

Jim Jones began the Peoples Temple as a Christian ***social action*** movement. He worked hard to include both black and white believers in his church, something almost unheard of at that time. The Peoples Temple provided a host of services for people who were homeless, jobless, and sick. They took in drug addicts and helped them recover. People from a wide variety of age groups and cultural backgrounds joined the movement, since it provided a way to build a better world and to enjoy a community based on love and equality.

At its height, the Peoples Temple had eight thousand members. Many of them failed to notice subtle signs that their idealistic church was becoming dangerous. In late 1976, negative reports began to come out of the Peoples Temple. Reporter Marshall Kilduff wrote a highly critical story about Jones, which he published in *New West* magazine in August of 1977. The article told how Jones faked healings, forced members to sell their homes, and made businesses hand over the money to the church.

In the 1970s, Jim Jones became increasingly concerned with the end times and the apocalypse. He said nuclear war would soon destroy the world; the United States was becoming corrupt, and society was going to collapse. His followers had to devote themselves even more to creating a perfect society that would survive the coming disasters. In 1974, the Peoples Temple leased four thousand acres of dense jungle from the government of Guyana, a small South American country. By 1977, most of the Peoples Temple had moved to Guyana. They called their colony Jonestown. Jones's followers raised cattle and tropical crops there.

GLOSSARY

incendiary: Containing highly flammable substances that will cause a fire on impact.

social action: Activity for the benefit of society.

By 1978, a number of Peoples Temple members had left the group. Concerned for the safety of friends and family members living with the group in Guyana, many of them contacted the U.S. government. U.S. Representative Leo Ryan, from California, flew to South America to visit the colony. As he was about to leave the country, assassins sent from Jonestown opened fire on Ryan, killing him and four of his companions. Meanwhile, back at the colony, more than nine hundred people met their deaths.

More than twenty years after the event, it is hard to know exactly what happened at Jonestown on that horrible day. The State Department has not released all of their records. The bodies were rotting when found, and workers buried them without careful examination. Only seven autopsies were performed. Many members died from drinking cyanide-laced Flavor-Aid. Others were shot. There are claims that some died from lethal injections. Former members of the Peoples Temple report that Jones made members practice drinking poison in

"Beloved, do not believe every spirit, but test the spirits to see if they are from God; for many false prophets have gone out into the word."

—the Apostle John

preparation for the end. He told his people they would be better off to "cross over to the other side" voluntarily, rather than allow evil society to destroy their religious way of life. Jim Jones died of a gunshot wound to the head.

In its early years, the Peoples Temple provided many helpful services for people in need. Jones received praise from many in government and even had his picture taken with First Lady Rosalyn Carter when she reportedly sought his support for her husband's presidential campaign. As Jim Jones became increasingly deceitful, controlling, and destructive, he talked more about the apocalyptic future. Jim Jones used frightening prophetic predictions to control and abuse people.

DAVID KORESH & THE BRANCH DAVIDIANS

In 1959, Vernon Wayne Howell was born in Houston, Texas. In the future, people would call him David Koresh. His fifteen-year-old single mother could not care for him. He never knew his father, and his grandparents raised him.

Vernon had a lonely childhood. Although he dropped out of high school, he had many talents, including musical skills and an outstanding memory for Bible verses. At the age of twenty, he was attending a Seventh Day Adventist church but was asked to leave because he was a bad influence on other young people.

In 1981, Howell went to Waco, Texas, where he joined the Branch Davidians, who had been there since 1935 as a "branch" or breakaway

group from the Seventh Day Adventist church. (The Adventists, a remnant group from Miller's Great Disappointment of 1843, have always been keenly interested in Bible prophecy.) The Branch Davidians focused on the book of Revelation. They believed it was their job to gather the 144,000 "servants of God" mentioned in Revelation 7. Once they did so, Christ would return.

Soon after joining the group, Howell had an affair with the leader of the group, the "prophetess" Lois Roden, a woman in her late sixties. When Lois Roden died, a power struggle began between Howell and Lois Roden's son George. In late 1987, Howell and several companions attacked Roden using automatic weapons. During the gunfight, someone shot Roden in the chest and hands. The government charged Howell and his followers with attempted murder. When the judge declared a mistrial, Howell was released.

By 1990, Vernon Howell had become the leader of the Branch Davidians. Claiming he was now head of the biblical House of David, Howell legally changed his name to David Koresh. (Koresh is the Hebrew version of Cyrus, the name of the Persian king who allowed the Jews held captive in Babylon to return to Israel.)

Koresh regarded himself as the Lamb from Revelation 5—an alias for Jesus Christ. He believed he would open the seven seals and interpret the scroll of destiny mentioned in Revelation 5:2. If he could accomplish this task, Koresh believed the end would come. Koresh decided it was his destiny to father a new race of God's children. He saw this as an important step in God's plan for the world, and in 1984, Koresh began taking "spiritual wives."

After establishing his leadership, Koresh changed the social structure of the Branch Davidians. They became much more communal. Koresh was inspiring and played Christian rock music, which helped to bring in more young people. Koresh and other leaders arranged marriages, and members had to give all their money to the leadership. A group of armed guards, called "The Mighty Men," controlled the members. Under Koresh, the Branch Davidians focused even more on the

The seventh seal
8 When the Lamb opene
seventh seal, there was sile
eaven for about half an hour.
saw the seven angels who sta
ore God, and seven trumpets
ven to them. 3And another
me and stood at the altar w
lden censer; and he was given
cense to mingle with the pray
l the saints upon the golden
fore the throne; 4 and the smo
e incense rose with the prayers
ints from the hand of the ang
re God. Then the angel took
nser and filled it with fire from
ar and
e earth
ere were
thunder, v
shes of lig
and an e
ake.
Now the seve
s who ha
en trumpets

"Nobody joins a cult. You join a self-help group, a religious movement, a political organization. They change so gradually, by the time you realize you're entrapped—and almost everybody does—you can't figure a safe way back out."

— Deborah Layton, a Peoples Temple member who survived the massacre

book of Revelation and the end of time. In an October 1989 tape recording, Koresh explained his sense of identity: "Do you know who I am? God in the flesh! I will be exalted among the heathen. Stand in awe and know that I am God."

In February of 1993, one hundred heavily armed agents of the Bureau of Alcohol, Tobacco, and Firearms (ATF) raided the Branch Davidian compound in Waco. They had a warrant to arrest Koresh. Authorities had charged him with stockpiling large amounts of illegal weapons. The Davidians saw the armed intruders as fulfillment of the Bible prophecies of Armageddon—the final battle between good and evil. Koresh and his followers fought the ATF agents with massive firepower. One correspondent said it "sounded like a war zone." Another reporter recalled, "There were people dropping left and right." After a forty-five-minute shoot-out, six ATF officers were dead and twenty more wounded. Six Davidians died.

For the next fifty-one days, FBI agents surrounded the Branch Davidian compound. There were many phone discussions between Koresh and the agents. Looking back at those days, some people have criticized the FBI for not understanding the sort of person with whom they were dealing. The government agents were thinking politically and strategically. Koresh was living in his own religious world of end-time Bible prophecy. Religious experts may have been able to negotiate more effectively with Koresh than the FBI agents could.

On April 19, the FBI made their final assault on the compound. Unknown to the government, this assault played almost perfectly on the prophetic delusions of Koresh and his followers. The government used tank-like combat engineering vehicles (CEVs) to punch holes in the compound wall—and for some time before the assault, Koresh had taught that evil world powers would attack the Christ (himself) at the Battle of Armageddon. At that time, Christ (Koresh) would cause the world to end in flame. His followers would then transform into fiery supernatural beings, able to destroy the enemies of Christ. He had also taught on Nahum 2:3–4: "The chariots shall be with flaming torches . . . the chariots shall rage in the streets" (KJV). Using a method of interpretation common among Bible prophecy teachers, Koresh had interpreted this passage so it would apply to modern times. He told his followers the chariots in this passage were tanks. As the CEVs bore down on the compound, Koresh and his followers waited for time to end in fiery judgment.

The final moments of the Branch Davidians are the subject of bitter and intense controversy. The basic facts are clear. Americans watched their TV sets in horror as the compound burst into flames. When the black smoke cleared from the Texas sky, seventy-five men, women, and children had died in the blaze. Government officials claim Koresh and his followers set the fire themselves. They may have done so to fulfill their understanding of Revelation. Others blame the FBI, claiming they shot ***incendiary*** devices into the compound. Still others claim the CEVs knocked over oil lamps.

The fiery inferno was not the end of Waco's bitter legacy. Two years later, Timothy McVeigh may have been seeking revenge over the Waco tragedy when he filled a Ryder truck with explosives and parked it in front of a government office building in Oklahoma City. The resulting explosion killed 168 people, many of them children attending a day-care center.

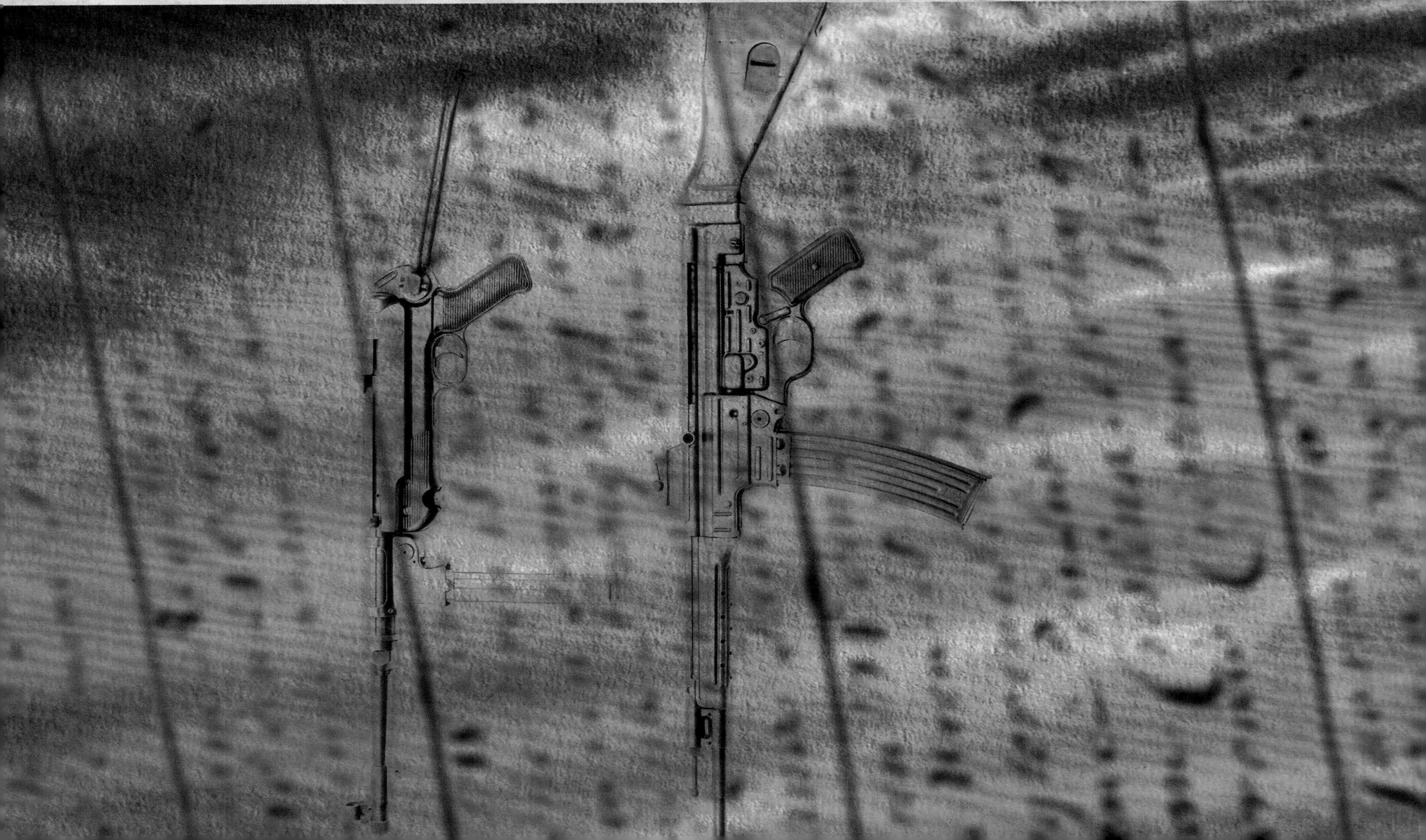

NINE CHARACTERISTICS OF CULTS OR DESTRUCTIVE RELIGIOUS GROUPS

How do we recognize a cult? Here are some characteristics. Not every cult has them all.

1. Each cult has a living leader who is charismatic, magnetic, and persuasive. Members regard this leader as a prophet or representative of the divine, but privately may worship this one as a god.
2. The leader claims special access to God, often through "new" scriptures.
3. The cult is deceptive in its recruiting and fund-raising techniques, often gathering personal information on members that can be used to keep them from leaving.
4. Each group has its own "devil" or phobia that members fear. Cult leaders manipulate devotees and hook deeply into feelings of guilt, shame and abandonment.
5. Outside information is tightly controlled. Members are cut off from family and friends.
6. Members are prohibited from interacting in meaningful ways, keeping them isolated and in pain.
7. Within the cult there is extreme rigidity and legalism regarding the "truth." Questions and doubts are suppressed, and members submit to the leader's authority.
8. Cults often disguise themselves from cult members and the public under the guise of political, economic, or military agendas.
9. A cult's ultimate goal is to remake members in the image of its leader.

[Quoted from Amy Schifrin, "Only the Names Have Changed, A Preview of Cults in the 90s," *Entrée*, February 1991.]

Before the end of the twentieth century, the United States saw yet another prophetic doomsday cult. On March 26, 1997, police in Rancho Santa Fe, California, received an anonymous phone call: "I think there was a religious group that committed suicide . . . I was notified by mail. I just thought I'd pass it on to you."

Hours later, police entered a sprawling mansion where they were met with the stench of death from thirty-nine corpses. Each body was dressed in black, lying on a mattress with hands at his or her side. All wore matching tennis shoes. Autopsies revealed they had drunk vodka laced with phenobarbital.

The dead were members of a religious group called Heaven's Gate. Their beliefs were a mixture of Bible prophecy, UFO lore, and science fiction. The founders of the group were Marshall Applewhite and Bonnie Lu Nettles (although they had changed their names to Ti and Do). Ti and Do claimed to be the two witnesses of Revelation 11. They believed in a place called "The Evolutionary Level Above Human" (TELAH), populated by aliens. According to Ti and Do, one of these aliens had possessed Jesus Christ, and a spaceship was coming soon to take Ti and Do's followers to TELAH.

Do and Ti had amazing charm and gained more than a thousand followers. They taught that believers must outgrow their individual humanity. Followers dressed in identical clothes, had identical haircuts, ate the same foods, and adopted similar-sounding names. They also abstained from sex.

Do and Ti had predicted that the "mother ship" would arrive in 1975 to take their followers home. When the ship failed to arrive, most of the Heaven's Gate followers left. However, a few of the faithful remained and became even more committed to the cause.

In 1996, Do and Ti believed their ship had arrived when the Hale-Bopp comet blazed across the nighttime sky. An amateur astronomer, Chuck Shramek, took a photo of the approaching comet. He claimed his photo showed "a large glowing object" following the comet. Heaven's

Gate members assumed this object was their long-expected spaceship. When the comet was closest to the earth, they drank their poison-laced vodka and laid down before leaving their "containers" (what they called their bodies).

EXCLUSIVE FOCUS ON END-TIME SPECULATIONS & DOOMSDAY CULTS

It would be easy to dismiss members of the Peoples Temple, the Branch Davidians, and Heavens Gate as "kooks" or loners. The facts don't fit that opinion. People of all sorts were in each of these groups. They included a significant number of educated people who left successful professional careers. Family and friends remembered them as "normal," healthy individuals.

Throughout history, doomsday cults have tried to legitimize themselves by focusing on Bible prophecy. The strange images and unexplained numbers found in the book of Revelation can fit with almost any belief. They are almost like the ink blots used by psychologists—one sees what one wishes. Chariots become tanks, the 144,000 become members of one's own cult, and so on.

By focusing exclusively on Bible prophecy, religious groups can avoid talking about other, more straightforward lessons found in their scriptures. In each of these groups, followers ignored basic Bible commandments like "you shall not kill" and "you shall not commit adultery."

Millions of Jews, Christians, and Muslims believe that God will end history. It is perfectly healthy to believe in fulfillment of ancient prophecies. Such beliefs are vital in almost every religion. Groups become unbalanced when believers focus exclusively on prophecy. They become dangerous when the emphasis on prophecy causes them to ignore other important beliefs—like love and the value of human life. Luckily, doomsday cults are very rare.

Chapter 5

NATIVE VISIONS & THE NEW AGE

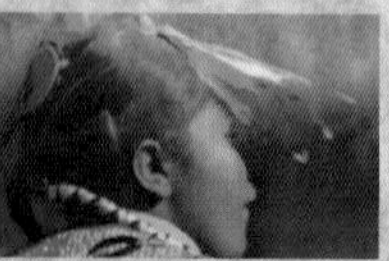

When Miracle Moon was born, Jim and Dena Riley knew she was no ordinary bison calf—but they could not have guessed that thousands of people would come to see this special creature. The Rileys had fallen in love with American buffalo and decided to raise them on their Wyoming ranch. On April 30, 1997, when a baby bison was born, another buffalo threw her and flipped her fifteen feet (4.5 meters) into the air. Jim was present at her birth and courageously placed himself between the adult bison and the baby to save its life. Amazingly, the baby was unhurt. That night was a full moon, and the Rileys named her Miracle Moon. However, many people feel the real miracle occurred days later.

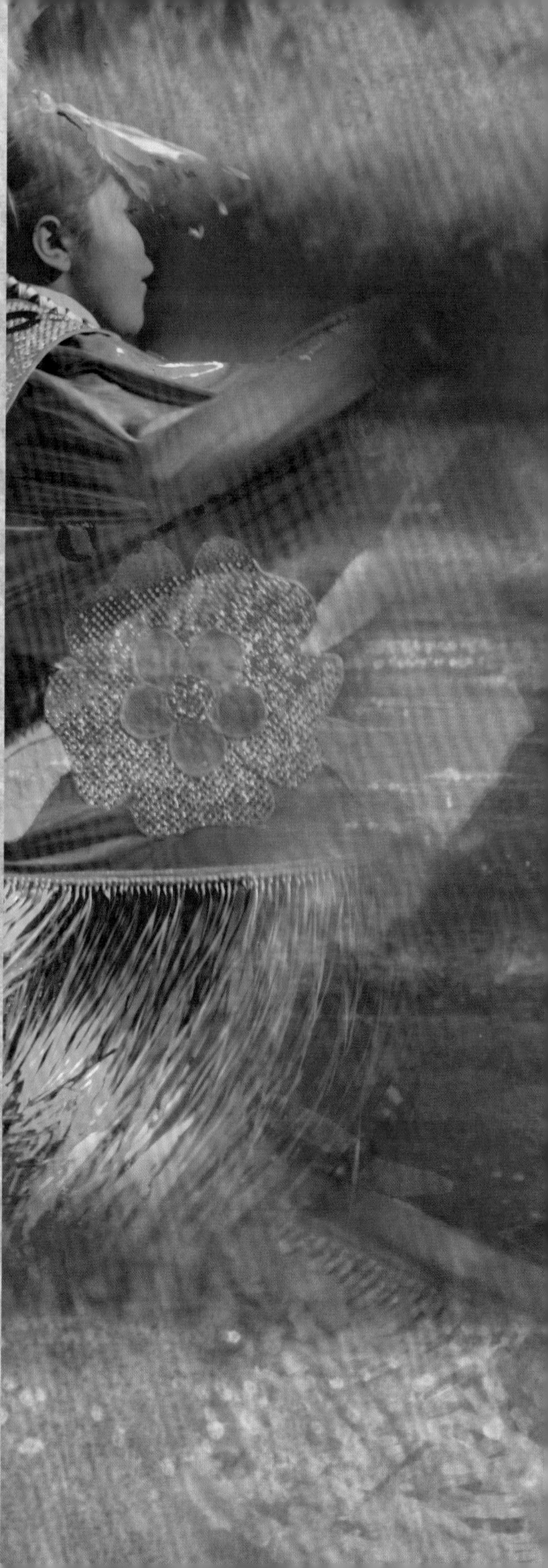

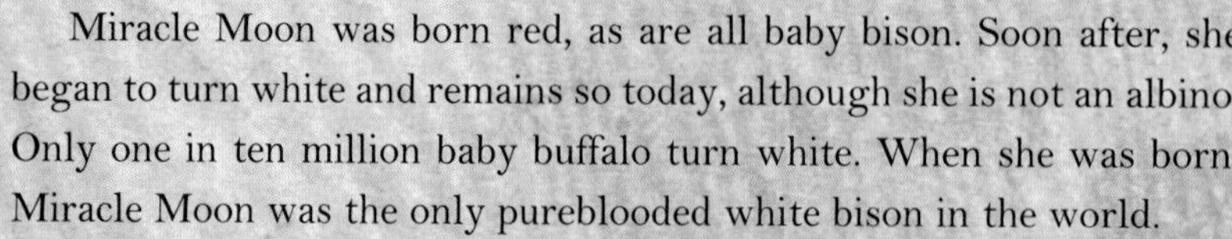

Miracle Moon was born red, as are all baby bison. Soon after, she began to turn white and remains so today, although she is not an albino. Only one in ten million baby buffalo turn white. When she was born, Miracle Moon was the only pureblooded white bison in the world.

She would be noteworthy as a highly unusual genetic occurrence, but American Indians believe Miracle Moon is something more important. For many Native people, the birth of a white buffalo signifies the fulfillment of ancient prophecy. The Lakota (Sioux) nation has retold the sacred tradition of the White Buffalo Woman since 1540.

According to tradition, two young men were out hunting when they saw a person in the distance. As they drew closer, they saw a beautiful young woman. One of the young men knew she was a sacred being and looked at her with respect. The other young man looked at her lustfully and reached out to take her sexually. A cloud covered the immoral young man, and when it cleared, his bones lay bare on the earth.

The young woman told the honorable young man to take a message to the people. She gave him sacred instructions to prepare for her coming to the camp. He brought her words to the people, who gladly did as she commanded. A few days later, the sacred woman came to the people. She was singing a beautiful song no one had ever heard before, and she carried a sacred bundle in her arms. She told the leaders, the men, women, and children how to behave with respect for one another, and how to live in harmony with all living things. Opening the bundle, she gave them the medicine pipe. She told them how to honor the pipe and how to use it to bring peace between people. She also explained the seven sacred ceremonies. According to some accounts, she promised to return a long time in the future, when a troubled land needed her to restore harmony. After the sacred woman had explained these things, she rose, walked clockwise within a circle, and left. The people watched as she exited the camp and then rolled over four times in the grass. When she stood again, she had become a white buffalo.

GLOSSARY

pueblos: Villages built by Native North or Central Americans in the southwestern United States.

shamans: People who act as go-betweens for the spiritual and physical worlds, and who are said to have powers of healing and prophecy.

The sacred bundle the white buffalo woman gave to the people is still with the Lakota nation in a sacred place on the Cheyenne River Indian Reservation in South Dakota. Arvol Looking Horse—the Keeper of the White Buffalo Calf Pipe—guards it. The Lakota have kept this sacred belief alive despite centuries of oppression by Europeans. To them, the unexpected appearance of a white buffalo calf seems a tangible sign of the Creator's favor. Jim and Dena Riley assert, "The Sacred White Buffalo come to us now when our mother, the Earth, is suffering. They bring us their gift of healing!"

Over the past seven years, the Rileys' bison have given birth to five more white calves. They have moved these special animals from Wyoming to Flagstaff, Arizona, and the Spirit Mountain Ranch. The ranch lies next to the San Francisco Peaks, which twenty-three different Native nations regard as sacred. Native groups perform traditional spiritual ceremonies atop the mountain.

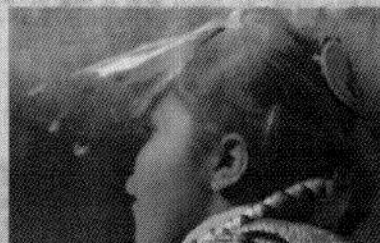

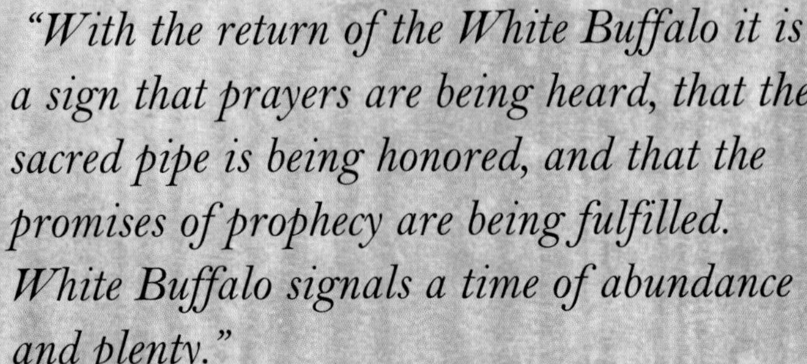

"With the return of the White Buffalo it is a sign that prayers are being heard, that the sacred pipe is being honored, and that the promises of prophecy are being fulfilled. White Buffalo signals a time of abundance and plenty."

—Jamie Sams and David Carson in Medicine Cards: The Discovery of Power Through the Ways of Animals

Thousands of people come to Spirit Mountain Ranch to see the white bison. Many are simply curious, some are skeptical, but a great many regard these creatures as true miracles from the Creator. They leave prayer ribbons and medicine pouches on the bison's fence—a way of showing respect for the creatures. Some visitors are Native Americans, but the majority are of other races. Many of them have accepted Native beliefs in the miracle of the white buffalo—a welcome sign of a coming happier age. According to the Rileys:

> Now, more than ever, recent events that are taking place worldwide are a wake-up call to seek connection to the divine Great Spirit or God that resides within us. The return of the White Buffalo is another physical sign from the world of Spirit, ready and waiting to help us walk in our world with wisdom, knowledge, peace and love.

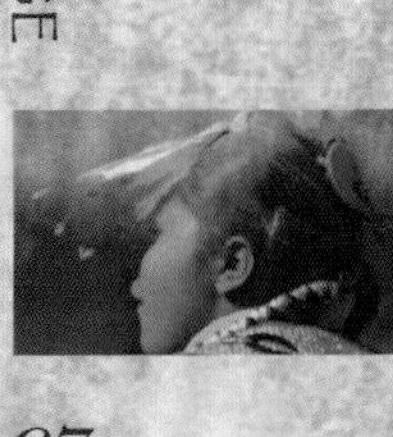

NATIVE PROPHECIES

In the twenty-first century, Americans practice a wide variety of spiritual beliefs. Some continue to practice Jewish and Christian faiths, but increasingly, citizens of the United States and Canada are exploring nontraditional religions such as Buddhism, Hinduism, Wicca, and Paganism. As part of this trend, Native beliefs have become popular among the non-Indian population, often to the chagrin of Native Americans. As Americans adopt spiritual beliefs outside Christianity and Judaism, they nonetheless continue to be fascinated with ancient prophecies of a coming future age.

A variety of Indian nations regard the modern-day world as the time for fulfillment of prophecy. Native prophetic beliefs differ in nature from those of Christians. While Christians forecast a sudden and catastrophic end to the age, accompanied by a final judgment, Native people forecast a more gradual change—the dawning of an age of healing, harmony, and restoration. They believe their ancient traditions contain the seeds of healing for nations that have misplaced their faith in technology. An important part of this change is giving honor to Mother Earth.

The number seven has special significance for many Indian nations. The Oceti Sakowin (Sioux), the People of the Seven Council Fires, speak of seven original people. The Haudenosaunee (Iroquois) say people must consider the effect of their actions on the seventh generation after them. Native Hawaiians also recall ancient prophecies of restoration in the seventh generation after the whites took over their lands. Many people, both of Native and non-Native heritage, regard today's youth as the prophesied seventh generation.

Other Native prophecies influence spiritual seekers today. Frank Waters' *The Book of the Hopi* contains a prophecy that has generated interest far away from the Hopi's desert home in Arizona:

ANCIENT END-TIME CALENDAR

Another influential Native prophecy is contained in the Maya calendar. The ancient Maya were excellent astronomers and mathematicians. They developed a highly complex calendar. According to this calendar, the world ends in December 2012.

> World War III will be started by those peoples who first received the light in the other old countries. The United States will be destroyed, land and people, by atomic bombs and radioactivity. Only the Hopis and their homeland will be preserved as an oasis to which refugees will flee. Bomb shelters are a fallacy. It is only materialistic people who make shelters. Those who are at peace in their hearts already are in the great shelter of life. . . . The time is not far off.

Pueblo Indians sometimes express anger at the ways non-Indians have adapted their traditional beliefs. Counterfeit Hopi ***shamans*** write books and charge money for seminars—and some of them do not even have a drop of Indian blood in their veins. Tourists flock to the ***pueblos***, trying to pry into private sacred matters. Despite the frustration of genuine Indian traditional leaders, spiritual seekers in the United States are increasingly imitating Indian beliefs and customs.

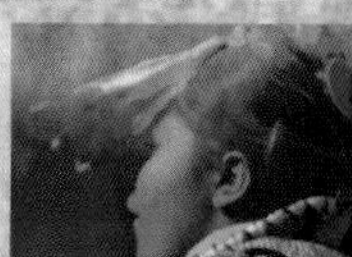

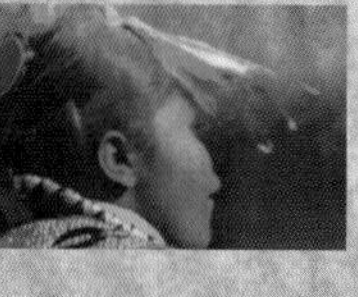

"The Red Nation shall rise again and it shall be a blessing for a sick world. A world filled with broken promises, selfishness and separations. . . . I see a time of Seven Generations when all the colors of humankind will gather under the Sacred Tree of Life and the whole Earth will become one circle again. In that day, there will be those among the Lakota who will carry knowledge and understanding of unity among all living things and the young white ones will come to those of my people and ask for this wisdom."

—*Chief Crazy Horse, four days before his assassination*

ASTROLOGY & THE NEW AGE

Native prophecies such as the Seventh Generation and the Maya calendar are believed to dovetail with astrological predictions from the ancient East. Astrology divides time into three ages: the age of Aries (the Ram) fits with Judaism, Pisces (the Fish) with Christianity, and Aquarius (the Water Bearer) with the New Age of rising spiritual awareness. The spring equinox (March 20) of the year 2000 began the Age of Aquarius. The beginning of the zodiac age of Aquarius coincided

NEW AGE NOT SO BIG IN CANADA AS IN THE UNITED STATES

The 2001 Canadian census found 1,525 people who reported their religion to be "New Age." That isn't many, compared with 68,000 reported in a U.S. survey that same year. However, this underestimates the influence of New-Age ideas in Canada. Many Canadians consider themselves Christian or identify themselves with other major religions, while incorporating New-Age concepts into their faith.

with an extraordinary planetary alignment. On May 5, 2000, the planets Mercury, Venus, Earth, Mars, Jupiter, and Saturn orbited into a straight line (more or less) with the Sun. Additionally, the Moon lined up between the Earth and Sun. Astrologers believe these events will bring in a New Age for humankind, hence the title sometimes applied to such beliefs: New Age spirituality. For some people, ancient Native prophecies, astrological forecasts, and the yearning for a better future combine to create the hope of a better world tomorrow.

Chapter 6

POP-CULTURE APOCALYPSE

In an instant, millions of people disappear.

At a wedding service, there are gasps of horror and astonishment from the guests. Holding hands before the altar, just before saying, "I do," the bride vanishes, and the groom clasps empty air in his trembling fingers.

Down the road, on a soft drink manufacturing plant's assembly line, soda cans begin to pile up against one another, clogging the conveyer belt. The supervisor yells, "Hey, Jim—what are you doing down there?" Jim doesn't hear him; he has dematerialized into thin air.

At a nearby hospital, a nurse walks through the row of plastic-covered baby cribs in a neonatal intensive care unit. Glancing up from the digital readout beside a crib, the nurse gasps. The infant is gone—and he was there just a moment ago. She looks at the next crib—empty. And the next—empty also. She screams and grabs the wall to steady herself. Every single baby in the unit is suddenly gone.

Outside on the freeway, cars careen off the road and smash into other vehicles. Their drivers have vanished. Getting out of their cars, shaken passengers phone 911, but there is no answer. The emergency lines are jammed—too many dispatchers have disappeared. Overhead, an airliner begins to tilt off course and then spin crazily toward the ground. Its pilot is gone. Walking from their vehicles, glancing in horror at the sky, people shudder and wonder: what is happening?

You may have seen a bumper sticker that reads, "WARNING, in case of Rapture this car will be unmanned." For the car's owner, the warning is probably no joke. The scenes described above are something that millions of Bible-believing Christians fully expect will actually happen, though millions more believe this is a misreading of scripture.

This event—the Rapture—is part of a complex set of beliefs based on an interpretation of the book of Revelation. That set of beliefs is the dispensational view of Bible prophecy. The *American Heritage Dictionary* defines "dispensation" as "the divine ordering of worldly affairs." Dispensationalists attempt to set forth God's plan for the world.

THE "LEFT BEHIND" PHENOMENA

Today, more people than ever before embrace dispensational views. This is due in large part to the *Left Behind* series of books discussed in chapter 1. The average reader of these books, according to a May 24,

GLOSSARY

Final Judgment: Standing before God to see where one will be spending eternity.

fundamentalism: A religious or political movement based on the literal interpretation and strict adherence to a doctrine.

2004, *Newsweek* article, is "a 44-year old born-again Christian woman, married with kids, living in the South." Yet Jews, agnostics, and atheists also read the books. For those who don't like to read, there is the movie and an upcoming TV show. For young readers, there is a teenage series. Huge numbers of people do not want to be left out when it comes to *Left Behind.*

Tim LaHaye had a hard life as a child. His family was poor, and his father died when he was ten. He recalls the funeral service:

> I was in despair. And the minister—I remember it as if it was yesterday—looked up at the sky and said, "This is not the end of Frank LaHaye. The day is going to come when Jesus will show himself and the dead will rise. And we who are alive in the Name will be caught up together in the clouds to meet the Lord in the air."

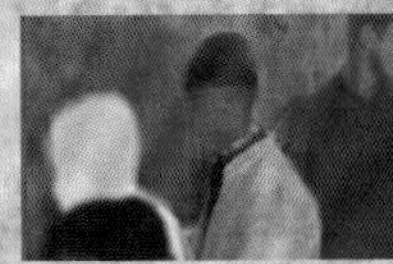

These words of comfort at his father's funeral have inspired Tim LaHaye to explain the Bible—especially the prophetic parts—ever since. His earnest faith keeps Tim LaHaye working hard. One friend says, "He lives on a golf course, and he plays maybe twice a year. He's too busy thinking, writing and praying."

LaHaye and Jenkins may be the most successful pair of coauthors in the history of publishing. They have an unusual style of working together. For each book in the *Left Behind* series, Tim LaHaye sends Jerry Jenkins a seventy- to one hundred-page outline describing the prophetic events to take place in the book. According to LaHaye, Jenkins "has the liberty to use his fictional gift to convey my message."

Jerry Jenkins says he was raised in "a good Christian home." His mother led him to a "personal relationship with Christ" when he was six years old. His father was a former marine and a police chief who Jenkins describes as "a man's man." Jenkins began writing about sports in his teens, and today he has written more than 150 books. He says, "I don't sing or dance or preach—that's all I do."

Like Tim LaHaye, Jerry Jenkins is serious about his Christian faith. He believes in the Bible and says, "We sort of have a responsibility to tell what it seems to say to us." Jenkins is an evangelical, but he allows himself to enjoy things that other evangelicals wouldn't approve. His favorite writer is Stephen King, whom some evangelicals refuse to read. Jenkins also likes Harry Potter, although some conservative Christians have accused the British fantasy series of promoting witchcraft. (Tim LaHaye considers the Harry Potter books to be propaganda for Black Magic.) Yet Jenkins defends his opinion by saying, "I love the *Wizard of Oz*, and I didn't want to grow up to be a witch."

Jenkins allows his characters to voice their questions and doubts regarding God and faith. Many readers can relate to that, although reviewers have criticized the *Left Behind* books for the ways God sometimes acts vengefully in the novels. In the *Newsweek* interview, Jenkins admitted his own discomfort with some of the things predicted in Bible prophecy. He says:

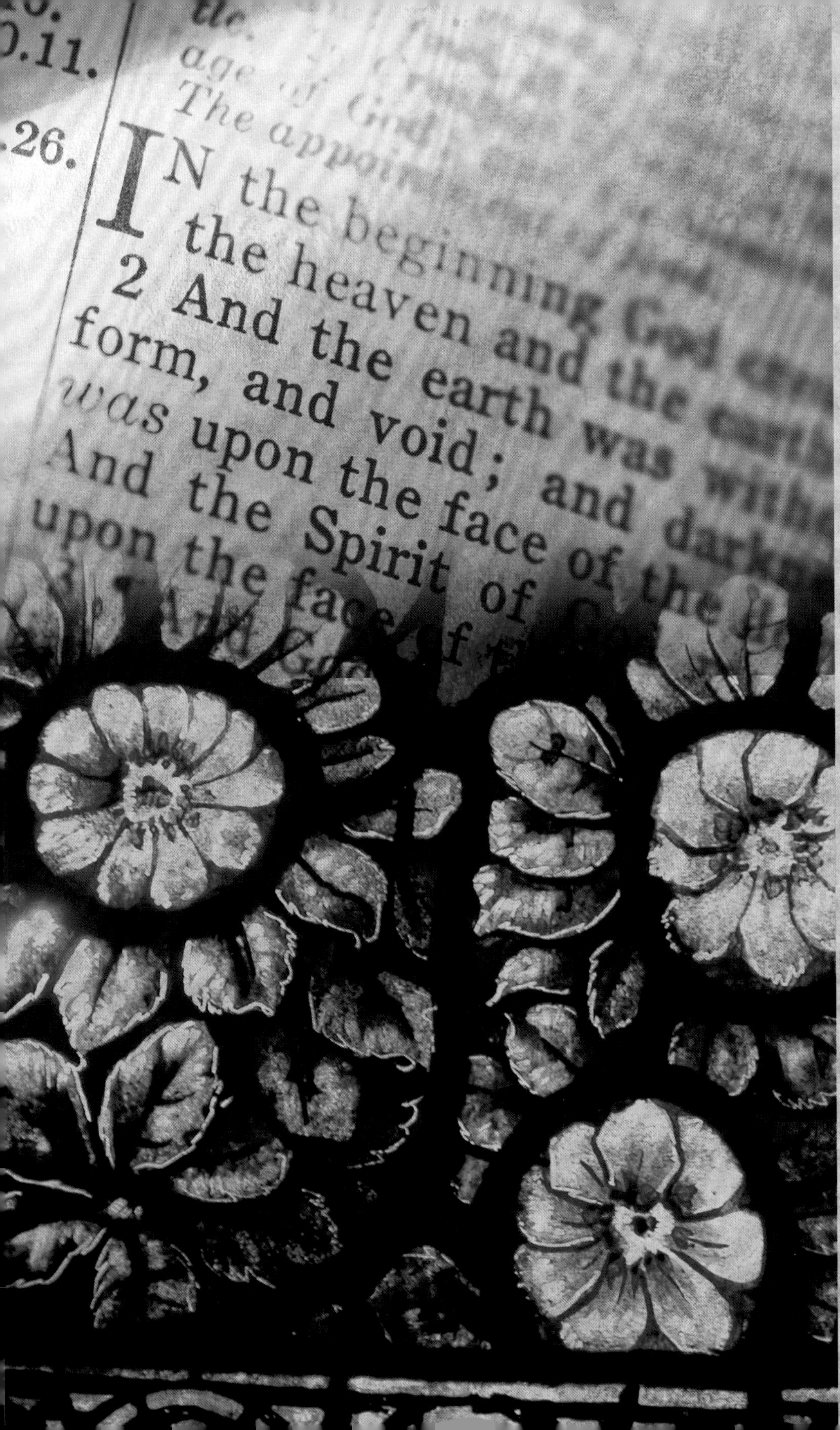

IN the beginning God
the heaven and the
2 And the earth was
form, and void; and
was upon the face of the
And the Spirit of
upon the face

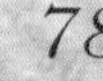

"Of making many books there is no end."

—Ecclesiastes, in the Hebrew Bible

To me there's a value in questioning, and even doubting sometimes. Chloe's big deal is, how does this sound like a loving God? People disappear, planes crash, people die—even people who might have believed, but it's too late. There is indication in the prophecies that God will harden some people's hearts. I don't get it myself; I don't understand how that fits in with God's plan. Yeah, those are hard things.

Not everyone agrees with LaHaye and Jenkins' dispensational approach to Bible prophecy. Randall Balmer, chairperson of the Religion Department at Barnard College, says, "It's pulp fiction based on a particular reading of the Bible. It diverts attention from the mandate of the New Testament to love God with all your heart and soul and mind and love your neighbor as yourself."

In spite of critics, LaHaye and Jenkins have inspired millions with their views of the Bible. They say more than three thousand people have become Christians due to their books. Most readers of the *Left Behind* novels believe Jesus is likely to return soon.

LaHaye and Jenkins, however, do not suggest a date for Christ's return. Tim LaHaye says, "We don't know when the Lord is going to come." He then quotes one of his favorite verses, Matthew 24:35: "Of that day and hour no one knows, no, not even the angels of heaven, but my Father only."

Shirtless and bare-footed men with long hair hold hands with girls wearing gauze skirts and flowers in their hair. Some lie on blankets smoking pot. Others sway to the music. On stage, a band with electric guitars and drums plays in front of a slowly oscillating psychedelic pattern. It is the summer of 1971. A time to love, get high, and listen to rock music.

A pair of earnest-looking longhairs walk onto the scene. They look a lot like ordinary hippies, but instead of peace signs they wear prominent wooden crosses. These guys are Jesus Freaks.

They walk over to a couple lounging on a blanket. One of them kneels down and speaks. "Hey, have you heard the good news? It won't be long now—Jesus is going to come back and put an end to all the wars and hunger and stuff going down here."

The girl on the blanket looks at him with surprise. She's a bit stoned, but she replies, "Jesus? No way, man."

The Jesus Freak just smiles back at her. "Yeah, really—there are ancient prophecies that tell all about it. Here, you can check it out for yourself." He hands her a paperback book with a bright red cover, titled *The Late Great Planet Earth.*

DARBY INVENTS DISPENSATIONALISM, SCOFIELD BRINGS IT TO AMERICA

The Jesus Freaks would have loved LaHaye and Jenkins' books. Today, many readers of the *Left Behind* series assume the views of LaHaye and Jenkins are a timeless way of interpreting the Bible. In fact, the dispensational view is a "Johnny-come-lately." It took 1,800 years of church history before someone came up with this prophetic scheme.

"We live in an era of millennial dreams. . . . Yet with each 'prophetic' date that turns out to be another workday, the fracture of faith is more painful."

—*Gershom Gorenberg,* The End of Days

John Nelson Darby (1800–1882), an Irish priest who converted to Protestant ***fundamentalism***, invented the dispensational interpretation of prophecy. Then, in 1909, C. I. Scofield published a new version of the Bible that influenced history and made Darby's dispensational ideas popular in America. For more than a century, Americans had been reading their Bibles and wondering, "What do all these strange symbols and numbers in Daniel and Revelation mean?" Scofield provided very practical help. His *Scofield Reference Version* of the King James Bible gave Darby's interpretations of each verse, printed right at the bottom of each page. Students of prophecy no longer had to wonder how to interpret Revelation—the answers were right in their Bibles. By the 1920s, Scofield had convinced most American fundamentalists of the dispensationalist view.

But what about those outside the fundamentalist movement? They had still not heard the dispensationalist view. It took Hal Lindsey to bring dispensationalist beliefs into popular American culture during the 1970s.

HAL LINDSEY MAKES END-TIME PROPHECY POPULAR

Harold Lindsey was born in Houston, Texas, in 1929. He dropped out of college to serve in the Korean War and later worked as a tugboat captain on the Mississippi River. When his marriage broke up, he wanted

to commit suicide—but a Gideon Bible in a hotel room saved his life. After reading the Bible, Lindsey committed himself to Christianity. He then devoted his life to studying and teaching the Bible. Although he had not finished college, he was able to obtain a seminary degree in the Bible due to his keen mind and interest. He remarried and went to work for Campus Crusade for Christ.

In the early 1970s, Lindsey published *The Late Great Planet Earth.* It was an immediate hit, selling more than thirty-five million copies in more than fifty different languages. There was also a film version of the book.

Lindsey took Darby and Scofield's dispensational map of the future and modernized it. When Darby studied the Bible a century before, references to Israel in the book of Revelation made little sense. Israel did not exist. The reestablishment of a Jewish State in the year 1948 gave Lindsey something more to go on.

Lindsey believed Jesus's words about "this generation," applied to the generation that saw Israel reestablished. A generation in the Bible is forty years, so it seemed Jesus would come around 1988. When that failed to happen, Lindsey changed his predictions. He decided "this generation" did not refer to the establishment of Israel in 1948, but to the Six Day War, which happened in 1967. So students of Hal Lindsey can reset their countdown to 2007.

Lindsey made Revelation hip. Chapters in *The Late Great Planet Earth* have catchy titles like, "Sheik to Sheik," "The Future Fuehrer," and "The Ultimate Trip." He invented a number of prophetic ideas that continue to influence Bible prophecy teachers today; for instance, the ancient nations of Gog and Magog in Ezekiel 38 are, according to Lindsey, Russia and China. Lindsey says the "myriads of myriads of horsemen" in Revelation 9 are the Chinese army. The "ten horns" of the dragon in Revelation 17 are the European Union. The whore Babylon is a combination of New-Age religion and the World Council of Churches. The plagues in Revelation are "an accurate first-century description of a twentieth-century nuclear war." Armageddon is an all-out nuclear holocaust.

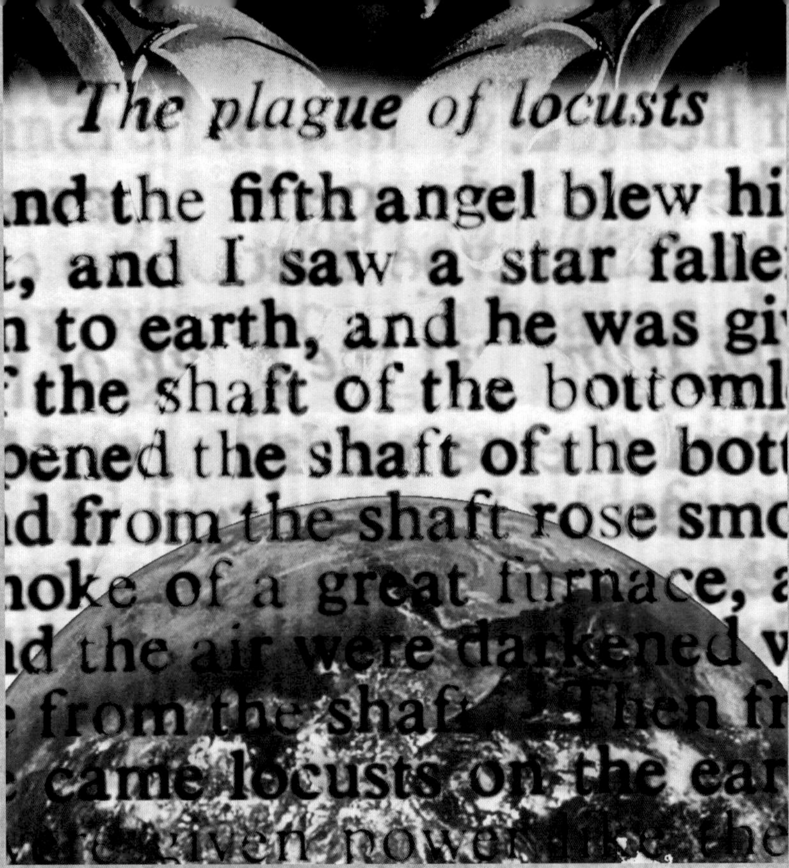

These modern-day interpretations of prophecy made Lindsey's book wildly popular. Dispensational ideas moved from the narrow boundaries of fundamentalism to the limitless expanse of American popular culture. People of all kinds were reading and talking about Bible prophecy.

EVANGELICALS, POLITICS, & PROPHECY

Evangelicals often allow Bible interpretation to influence their political views. Dispensationalist evangelicals, for example, are uncritical and committed supporters of Israel. As a result, Christian Zionism—unconditional support for Israel by evangelicals—has increased in the first years of the twenty-first century. Dispensationalists believe anyone opposing the modern Jewish state is opposing God. Hence, they have little sympathy for Palestinians who claim to suffer wrong from Israel.

As far back as 1970, Hal Lindsey pointed out there was "one major problem" preventing the return of Christ—the Dome of the Rock atop

AVOID STEREOTYPES!

When thinking about religious groups and ideas, stereotypes often obscure the truth. Christians in the United States hold to a great variety of beliefs. Some Catholics are liberal Christians, while others are very conservative; some evangelicals are politically liberal; and some religious fence-sitters hold dispensational views (at least to some degree). There are also conservative Christian evangelicals who do not agree at all with the dispensational view of prophecy. Many Americans are uncertain what they believe, or why. They find the *Left Behind* books interesting but not necessarily persuasive. The popular view of Revelation found in LaHaye and Jenkins' books is an important part but still only a part of some Americans' end-time beliefs.

the location of Solomon's Temple in Jerusalem. He assures his readers, "Obstacle or no obstacle, it is certain the Temple will be rebuilt. Prophecy demands it." Likewise, according to Lindsey's view, the Arab nations only have a negative role in God's plans for history.

Dispensational beliefs also influence environmental issues. Right-wing Christians are the voters most likely to be unconcerned with preserving the environment—and the same citizens are likely to hold dispensational prophetic views. If fiery judgments are going to obliterate the environment during the tribulation, as dispensationalists believe, why waste time recycling and cutting down on pollution?

Dispensationalists such as LaHaye and Jenkins have worked out a complicated road map of future prophetic events. Because so many people believe in this outline of the future, it is worthwhile to understand their predictions (whether or not you believe them). But the dispensational road map of the future is not simple.

The first event of the dispensational end-times calendar is the Rapture. As discussed previously, the word "Rapture" means "to be caught up" by something or someone. The phrase "caught up" occurs once in the Bible, in the Apostle Paul's first letter to the Thessalonians: "Then we who are alive, who are left, will be caught up in the clouds . . . to meet the Lord in the air; and so we will be with the Lord forever" (1 Thessalonians 4:17).

Following the Rapture, the Antichrist appears. Dispensationalists combine the description of "the Beast" in Revelation chapter 13 and the "Man of Lawlessness" in 2 Thessalonians chapter 2 to create a composite picture of the Antichrist. According to LaHaye and Jenkins, the Antichrist is a:

> leader of humanity who may emerge from Europe. He will turn out to be a great deceiver who will step forward with signs and wonders that will be so impressive that many will believe he is of God . . . I warn you to beware now of a new leader with great charisma trying to take over the world during this terrible time of chaos and confusion. This person is known in the Bible as the Antichrist.

The Rapture and the Antichrist's first appearance are followed by seven years of woe known as the Tribulation. LaHaye and Jenkins describe this as well: "The Bible teaches that the Rapture of the church

PIN THE TAIL ON THE ANTICHRIST

Over the past decades, dispensationalists have nominated a number of unwilling candidates as possibly being the Antichrist. Adolf Hitler was an obvious choice. Mikhail Gorbachev, Henry Kissinger, Pope John Paul II, and Ronald Reagan are among the more surprising candidates. Like the Beast in Revelation 13, both the pope and Reagan were wounded in an assassination attempt, yet survived. Reagan's full name—Ronald Wilson Reagan—has six letters in each part, and the number of the Antichrist in Revelation is 666. In the *Left Behind* books, the Antichrist is a fictional politician named Nicolae Carpathia from Romania.

ushers in a seven-year period of trial and tribulation, during which terrible things will happen." The word "tribulation" appears in Matthew's Gospel and the book of Revelation.

After the Great Tribulation comes the battle of Armageddon—the final showdown between good and evil: "Demonic spirits . . . go abroad to the kings of the whole world, to assemble them for battle on the great day of God the Almighty. . . . And they assembled them at the place that

92

RELIGION & MODERN CULTURE

in Hebrew is called Armageddon" (Revelation 16:14–16). Hal Lindsey explains, "According to the Bible, the Middle East crisis will continue to escalate until it threatens the peace of the whole world." Increased conflict between Israel and her neighbors leads to World War III and nuclear annihilation.

Armageddon is not the end of the world, because in the middle of the battle, Jesus returns in glory. Bible scholars describe Jesus's second coming as the Parousia, the New Testament Greek word for "arrival."

Immediately after this is the ***Final Judgment***, when the book of Matthew says Jesus will declare,

> Come, O blessed of my father, inherit the Kingdom prepared for you . . . for I was hungry and you gave me food, I was thirsty and you gave me drink, I was a stranger and you welcomed me, I was naked and you clothed me, I was sick and you visited me, I was in prison and you came to me. (Matthew 24:35–36, RSV)

Jesus's followers are confused: "When did we do all these things?" Jesus replies, "Whatever you did to the least of my brothers and sisters you did for me."

As you follow the dispensational road map of the future, still more takes place on earth after the Final Judgment. Now the Millennium comes. This belief is based on Revelation 20:1–6: "An angel . . . seized Satan . . . and bound him for a thousand years." During that same time, "I saw the souls of those who had been beheaded for their testimony to Jesus . . . they came to life and reigned with Christ for a thousand years."

Finally, after the Millennium, comes the "new heaven and new earth" described in Revelation chapters 21 and 22. Heaven and Earth become one, and God restores all good things:

> Now the dwelling of God is with human beings, and he will live with them. They will be his people, and God himself will be with them and be their God. He will wipe every tear from their eyes. There will be no more death or mourning or crying or pain, for the old order of things has passed away. (Revelation 21:3–5, NIV).

Chapter 7

REVELATION REVISITED

Swoosh! The long arm of a Roman catapult swings up into the sky. A great rock, weighing more than a hundred pounds, soars through the air. It flies over the battered stone ramparts of ancient Jerusalem and comes smashing down through the tile roof of a wealthy citizen's house. As the ground shakes and dust flies from the impact, the occupants of the house utter screams and cries of agony.

Within the walls of Jerusalem, a million men, women, and children cower during the final holdout for Israel. For three and a half years, Jews and Romans have fought. Now, the Romans have pushed them back into the Holy City.

THE

REVELATION TO JOHN

(The Apocalypse)

The source of the revelation

The revelation of Jesus Christ,
which God gave him to show to his
ervants what must soon take place;
nd he made it known by sending his
ngel to his servant John, [2] who bore
itness to the word of God and to the
estimony of Jesus Christ, even to all
hat he saw. [3] Blessed is he who reads
loud the words of the prophecy, and
[illegible] who hear, and who
[illegible] for the
[illegible]

[illegible] churches that
[illegible]

ing I saw seven golden lampstands,
[13] and in the midst of the lampstands
one like a son of man, clothed with a
long robe and with a golden girdle
round his breast; [14] his head and his
hair were white as white wool, white as
snow; his eyes were like a flame of fire,
[15] his feet were like burnished bronze,
refined as in a furnace, and his voice
was like the sound of many waters;
[16] in his right hand he held seven stars,
from his mouth issued a sharp two-
edged sword, and his face was like the
sun shining in full strength.
[illegible]

him who loves us a
[illegible] our sins by his
made us a kingdom, priest
and Father, to him be g
forever and ever
[illegible] coming with the
[illegible] see him, e
[illegible]

Each day, huge stones fly into the city. These missiles even crash into the courts of the Great Temple. Temple priests continue their sacrifices through the bombardment. As the Jewish historian Josephus, who was alive at the time, recalls, "Those who had journeyed from all over the world to worship there sprinkled the altar with their own blood."

The armies of General Titus have surrounded the city for more than four months. No food comes into the city, and the people are starving. Josephus recalls, "The poor starved to death by thousands. People gave all their wealth for a little measure of wheat, and hid it hastily. . . . Wives would snatch the food from their husbands, children from fathers, and mothers from the very mouths of infants." Josephus also says, "The sufferings of the people were so fearful that they can hardly be told, and no other city ever endured such miseries."

Finally, in September, the Romans smash through the city walls with battering rams. Blood flows in the streets. Soldiers slaughter old men, wives, children; they butcher people indiscriminately. More than a million Jewish people die in one hellish day; 97,000 are left alive so the Romans can make an example of them. These Jews spend their lives in harsh slavery or are tortured to death or killed for amusement in Rome's arena. The fall of Jerusalem in 70 CE is the first holocaust—the horrific end of the ancient nation of Israel. It is one of the worst slaughters in world history, even though it occurred prior to the development of weapons of mass destruction during the twentieth century.

THE PRETERIST VIEW OF BIBLE PROPHECY

According to a growing number of Bible scholars, the fall of Jerusalem in 70 CE—along with the persecution of Christians by the Emperor Nero—is the real subject of the book of Revelation. Those who hold this view are *preterists,* a word that comes from the Latin word meaning "gone by" or "past." Where dispensationalists read Revelation as a map

A DREAM FOR THE FUTURE FOUNDED ON ANCIENT WORDS OF HOPE

Look at Dr. Martin Luther King's "I Have a Dream" speech. The words of the prophet Isaiah and of Matthew's Gospel come to life again in the prophetic voice of Dr. King.

> *"I have a dream today. I have a dream that one day* every valley shall be exalted, every hill and mountain shall be made low, the rough places will be made plain, and the crooked places will be made straight, and the glory of the Lord shall be revealed, and all flesh shall see it together. *This is our hope. This is the faith with which I return to the South. With this faith we will be able to hew out of the mountain of despair a stone of hope. With this faith we will be able to transform the jangling discords of our nation into a beautiful symphony of brotherhood. With this faith we will be able to work together, to pray together, to struggle together, to go to jail together, to stand up for freedom together, knowing that we will be free one day."*

"As he came near and saw the city [Jerusalem] he wept over it, saying, 'If you . . . had only recognized the things that make for peace! . . . the days will come upon you, when your enemies will set up ramparts. . . . They will crush you to the ground, you and your children within you."

—words of Jesus in Luke's Gospel

Preterists note numerous Bible verses that talk about important events in prophecy happening in the time of the first hearers. In Matthew chapter 24, Jesus says, "Truly I say to you, this generation will not pass away until all these things take place." The opening verse of Revelation says, "The revelation of Jesus Christ which God gave him to show his servants what must soon take place."

Preterists believe the "Great Tribulation" is the time when Nero persecuted believers and Rome warred against Jews in the first century. Jesus speaks of "the great tribulation" in Matthew 24 as the time of "the end." Preterists believe this is the end of Jerusalem—not the end of the world. In the same place, Jesus told Christians, "flee to the mountains" when these things happen. Christians in 70 CE did just as Jesus said—they ran from the besieged city to the mountain city of Pella in Jordan. Thus, most Christians survived the slaughter when Jerusalem fell.

Revelation mentions two time periods that make up the Great Tribulation, each lasting three and a half years. Revelation 13:5 says for three and a half years of tribulation, "the beast" will "make war on the saints and conquer them." Many Bible scholars believe Nero is "the beast" of Revelation. He persecuted Christians from November 64 CE to June of 68 CE, and preterists point out that this accords perfectly with the three and a half years in Revelation.

You may ask, "Why weren't these things stated more clearly?" For a good understanding of the preterist answer, read Hank Hanegraaff's novel *The Last Disciple*, which tells a dramatic story about Christians living in Rome during the time of Nero. These Christians must keep the interpretation of John's Revelation secret because the psychopathic emperor has spies everywhere. According to the novel, the "number of the beast" is the name Nero—in code based on the Hebrew language.

Three and a half years is also the time Revelation says that "Gentiles will trample the Holy City" (11:2). Preterists point out that Roman armies first attacked Jerusalem in the spring of 67 CE, and they finished the job three and a half years later. Descriptions of the plagues during the tribulation fit with the Romans' war against the Jews. Revelation 16 describes how "great hailstones, heavy as a hundred weight, dropped on

100

RELIGION & MODERN CULTURE

men from heaven, till men cursed God for the plague of hail." Preterists recall the hundred-pound, white-colored stones thrown from Roman catapults into Jerusalem during the siege.

Preterists do not believe all of Revelation has been fulfilled, however. There is still the second coming of Jesus. Most preterists believe the very final events in Revelation 20–22 are still to come. They look forward to some unknown day when the final trumpet will sound, Jesus will return, and history will end. Unlike many dispensationalists, preterists do not look at world events in the newspaper as "clues" to when that time will come. According to them, the Great Tribulation and the Antichrist have already come—long ago.

THE APOCALYPSE IN AN AFRICAN AMERICAN CHURCH

Recently, an African American pastor preached in a big-city church, using text from Revelation 7 as his focus: "After this I looked, and behold, a great multitude which no man could number, from every nation, from all tribes and peoples and tongues, standing before the throne." In the verses that follow, John asks an angel, "Who are these?" and the angel replies, "These are they who have come out of the great tribulation."

The pastor declared, "These are the ones who have come out of great tribulation. Sisters and brothers, we *know* tribulation." The congregation responded, "Uh-huh . . . that's right." He repeats, "We *know* tribulation." The congregation agrees with him, even more vigorously.

For this church, the tribulation is not some forecasted frightening future event. It certainly is not something that happened back in the first century. Tribulation is what people experience now. Tribulation is when someone will not hire you because of your skin color. Tribulation is trying to raise a family with limited income and poor public services.

Tribulation is when family members make unwise choices and suffer as a consequence. There is nothing theoretical about Revelation for these people; they are practicing an idealist interpretation of Revelation.

THE IDEALIST VIEW OF REVELATION

The Idealist approach is another way to read Revelation. Idealist interpreters see Revelation as a metaphor for what happens all the time in life. There is always Great Tribulation because this world is always hos-

"All shall be well, and all shall be well. And all manner of things shall be well."

— Julian of Norwich, fourteenth-century mystic

tile to people of faith. There is always an antichrist (in fact, John's first letter says there are "many antichrists"). Nero, Napoleon, Hitler, Stalin, Osama bin Laden—these were all crazy leaders who persecuted people. So the instructions in Revelation do not solely address first-century believers, and they are not just addressed to the last generation of believers either. They are for believers in every age.

This Idealist view is compatible with other methods of interpretation. Whether the words apply to the past or the future, most religious readers believe sacred scriptures speak directly to them.

END-TIME BELIEFS & HOPEFUL LIVES

Belief in end-time prophecies gives many people a sense of hope and confidence to face their daily troubles. In *The Last Disciple*, the Apostle John says, "I'm sure that all believers would wish to be whisked away . . . to avoid the Tribulation. Yet that would be a false hope, especially if it replaces the true hope of the resurrection, for the resurrection of Jesus . . . gives us hope to endure troubles." In the Hebrew Bible, the prophet Isaiah speaks in apocalyptic language. At the same time, he speaks clearly about how his words should influence hearers. "Comfort, comfort my people, says your God" (Isaiah 40:1). Young Native Americans find hope in the prophecies that they are the Seventh Generation—the ones who will restore harmony to the earth. Believers in the coming astrological New Age say their lives are more peaceful and focused. Abdul Yusuf Ali says the Koran tells Muslims, "Various are the ways of work-

ing we see in Allah's world . . . through it all runs a Purpose True and stable, which we all shall see fulfilled on the Day of Judgment and Justice, which must inevitably come to pass." Hope in God's future gives many people in the present world hope.

Hope in God's future gives some people more than hope—it drives them to create that future. Ancient words predicting a future of peace and justice inspired Martin Luther King Jr., César Chávez, and other men and women of faith to make a better world. People of faith continue to pursue the dream of a future where, "They shall beat their swords into plowshares, and their spears into pruning hooks; nation shall not lift up sword against nation, neither shall they learn war nay more . . . and none shall make them afraid, for the mouth of the Lord . . . has spoken" (Micah 4:3–4).

FINAL JUDGMENT

You may be thinking, "Yes, end-time beliefs can comfort and inspire. Don't they frighten people as well? What about all those predictions of Final Judgment—those don't sound very comforting."

In all three monotheistic (one-God) faiths, a Final Judgment is predicted. In the Hebrew Bible Joel predicts a gathering of "Multitudes, multitudes, in the valley of decision! For the day of the Lord is near in the valley of decision" (Joel 3:14). Jesus promised a day when he would sit on his throne and separate all people as a shepherd separates the sheep from the goats (Matthew 25). The Koran predicts, "When one blast is sounded on the trumpet, and the earth is moved and its mountains, and they are crushed to powder at one stroke. . . . That day shall ye be brought to judgment; not an act of yours that ye hide will be hidden" (Surah 69:13–18).

All three faiths contain the assumption that Final Judgment is based on what people have done during their lifetimes. Judaism generally agrees that God rewards the keeping of his commandments. Prayer, repentance, and *tzedakah* (doing good to others) please God when he considers reward. In the Christian scriptures, Jesus tells his followers, "Whatever you did for the least of these"—people in jail, in hunger, and in poverty—"you did for me." In Islam, prayer, fasting, and charity are the habits that Allah will reward on the Final Day.

Most evangelical Christians believe somewhat differently from other monotheists regarding the basis of Judgment. They focus on the importance of Jesus's death in making a way to God. Thus, Final Judgment for evangelicals depends on whether one has accepted Christ's death as a substitute for one's punishment for personal sins. In the Final Judgment, God declares "not guilty" those who have trusted in his Son. "If you confess . . . Jesus is Lord. . . . You will be saved" (Romans 10:9). Yet even these evangelicals agree with the book of James that "faith without works is dead"; in other words, those who profess Christ as Lord will want to show his love to others.

While Final Judgment may be frightening for some, it is comforting for others. Final Judgment means there will finally be justice. Evil men, like Hitler, have died without suffering appropriately for the terrible pain they inflicted on others. In this world, people are often denied justice. Belief in Final Judgment assures people of faith that justice will not be denied forever.

In every culture and every age, people have yearned for a world that is "just right." The experiences of life leave us wishing for somewhere better. In almost all major religions, the final product of the Universe is a renewed world where peace and justice reign. If there is judgment, its purpose is to finally remove or purify all evil from the world. The end of everything is, to quote Oxford professor and Christian philosopher C. S. Lewis, "the Great Story, which no one on earth has ever read: which goes on for ever: in which every chapter is better than the one before."

FURTHER READING

Abanes, Richard. *End Time Visions: The Doomsday Obsession,* Nashville, Tenn.: Broadman & Holman, 1998.

Bell, James, and Stan Campbell. *The Complete Idiot's Guide to the Book of Revelation.* Indianapolis, Ind.: Alpha, 2002.

Brouwer, Sigmund, and Hank Hanegraaff. *The Last Disciple.* Wheaton, Ill.: Tyndale House, 2004.

Gregg, Steve. *Revelation: Four Views: A Parallel Commentary.* Nashville, Tenn.: Thomas Nelson, 1997.

Heard, Alex. *Apocalypse Pretty Soon: Travels in End-Time America.* New York: W. W. Norton, 1999.

Hendriksen, William. *More than Conquerors: An Interpretation of the Book of Revelation.* Grand Rapids, Mich.: Baker House, 1998.

Holy Bible, New Revised Standard Version. Nashville, Tenn.: Thomas Nelson, 1989.

Jenkins, Jerry B., and Tim LaHaye. *Left Behind: A Novel of the Earth's Last Days.* Wheaton, Ill.: Tyndale House, 1995.

Lindsey, Hal. *The Late Great Planet Earth.* Grand Rapids, Mich.: Zondervan, 1970.

FOR MORE INFORMATION

Endtime
www.endtime.com/

End-time Prophecies: A Catholic Perspective
www.conventhill.com/endtimes/

Planet Preterist
planetpreterist.com/

Red White Blue & Brimstone
www.lib.virginia.edu/small/exhibits/brimstone/

Religious Movements Homepage at the University of Virginia
religiousmovements.lib.virginia.edu

Revelation
www.apocalipsis.org/

Revelation Ministry
www.pioneer-net.com/~revmin/

Spirit Mountain Ranch
www.sacredwhitebuffalo.org/

Publisher's note:
The Web sites listed on this page were active at the time of publication. The publisher is not responsible for Web sites that have changed their addresses or discontinued operation since the date of publication. The publisher will review and update the Web-site list upon each reprint.

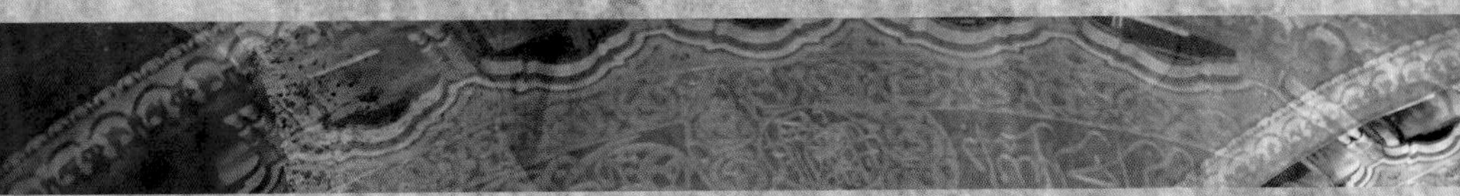

INDEX

Abanes, Richard 12, 39
African American beliefs 101–102
ancient prophecies 18–29
apocalyptic books 21–22
Ark of the Covenant 20, 21
astrology 70–71
Augustine 32–33

Black Death 33, 35
Book of Revelation 21, 22, 25, 26, 29, 32, 33, 35, 43, 50, 53, 58, 74, 96, 98, 99, 101–102
Branch Davidians 49–50, 53

Canadian beliefs 17, 71
Cayce, Edgar 12
Christian beliefs 20, 104, 107

date setting 13, 15–16, 36
dispensational beliefs 74–76, 79, 83, 86–88, 91, 93, 96
Dome of the Rock 18, 20, 86
doomsday cults 44–61
  characteristics of 57

Final Judgment 104, 107
fundamentalism 83

"The Great Disappointment" 36, 50

Heaven's Gate 58, 61
Holy of Holies 20

Idealist view 102–103

Jehovah's Witnesses 36, 40
Jerusalem 94, 96, 98
Jesus Freaks 80
Jewish beliefs 20, 104, 107

King, Dr. Martin Luther 97, 104
The Late Great Planet Earth 40, 80, 83–84
Left Behind series 8, 10, 12, 74–75, 79–80, 87, 91
Lindsey, Harold 40, 83–84, 86, 93
Luther, Martin 35

Middle Ages 32–33, 35–36
millenialists 30, 32
Miller, William 36, 40, 50
Miracle Moon 62–64, 66
Muslim beliefs 20, 104, 107

Native prophecies 68–70
Nero 26, 96, 98, 99
New Age spirituality 70–71
Nostradamus 12, 35, 39

Oklahoma City bombing 54
Old Testament 21, 25

The Peoples Temple 44, 46–47, 49
preterists 96, 98–99, 101

Raiders of the Lost Ark 20
the Rapture 10, 74, 88
the Reformation 35
Russell, Charles Taze 40

second coming of Christ predictions 40, 43

Torah 21

White Buffalo Woman stories 64–65

PICTURE CREDITS

The illustrations in Religion and Modern Culture are photo montages made by Dianne Hodack. They are a combination of her original mixed-media paintings and collages, the photography of Benjamin Stewart, various historical public-domain artwork, and other royalty-free photography collections.

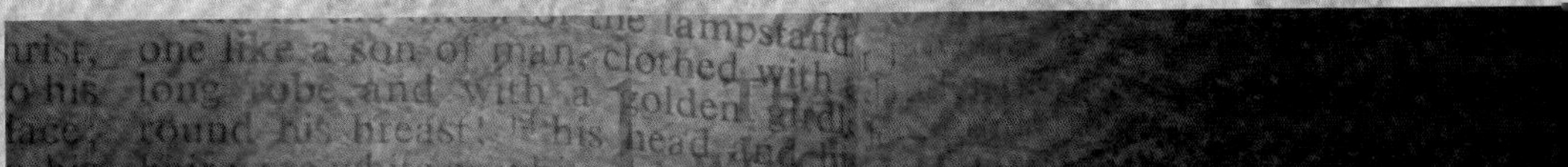

BIOGRAPHIES

AUTHOR: Kenneth McIntosh is a freelance writer living in Flagstaff, Arizona, with his wife Marsha, nineteen-year-old son Jonathan, and sixteen-year-old daughter Eirené—along with two cats and a dog. He formerly spent a decade teaching junior high in inner-city Los Angeles. He enjoys hiking, boogie boarding, and vintage Volkswagens. He has a bachelor's degree in English and a master's degree in theology. Ken has traveled and studied in the Holy Land and has spent much time studying the book of Revelation.

CONSULTANT: Dr. Marcus J. Borg is the Hundere Distinguished Professor of Religion and Culture in the Philosophy Department at Oregon State University. Dr. Borg is past president of the Anglican Association of Biblical Scholars. Internationally known as a biblical and Jesus scholar, the *New York Times* called him "a leading figure among this generation of Jesus scholars." He is the author of twelve books, which have been translated into eight languages. Among them are *The Heart of Christianity: Rediscovering a Life of Faith* (2003) and *Meeting Jesus Again for the First Time* (1994), the best-selling book by a contemporary Jesus scholar.

CONSULTANT: Dr. Robert K. Johnston is Professor of Theology and Culture at Fuller Theological Seminary in Pasadena, California, having served previously as Provost of North Park University and as a faculty member of Western Kentucky University. The author or editor of thirteen books and twenty-five book chapters (including *The Christian at Play*, 1983; *The Variety of American Evangelicalism*, 1991; *Reel Spirituality: Theology and Film in Dialogue*, 2000; *Life Is Not Work/Work Is Not Life: Simple Reminders for Finding Balance in a 24/7 World*, 2000; *Finding God in the Movies: 33 Films of Reel Faith*, 2004; and *Useless Beauty: Ecclesiastes Through the Lens of Contemporary Film*, 2004), Johnston is the immediate past president of the American Theological Society, an ordained Protestant minister, and an avid bodysurfer.